-25

D0481301

Dangerous Ground

UINTA COUNTY LIBRARIES
EVANSTON BRANCH
701 MAIN ST
EVANSTON, WY 82930

Dangerous Ground

GLORIA SKURZYNSKI

Bradbury Press
New York

UINTA COUNTY LIBRARIES
EVANSTON BRANCH
701 MAIN ST.
EVANSTON, WY 82930
90 4048

"When It's Springtime in the Rockies," composed by Robert
Sauer and Mary Hale Woolsey. © 1923 ROBERT SAUER
© 1929 VILLA MORET, INC. Copyright Renewed 1951, 1957
ROBBINS MUSIC CORPORATION
All Rights of ROBBINS MUSIC CORPORATION
Assigned to SBK CATALOGUE PARTNERSHIP
All Rights Controlled and Administered by
SBK ROBBINS CATALOG INC.
International Copyright Secured
Made In U.S.A.
All Rights Reserved

Copyright © 1989 by Gloria Skurzynski
All rights reserved. No part of this book may be reproduced
or transmitted in any form or by any means, electronic or
mechanical, including photocopying, recording, or by any
information storage and retrieval system, without permission
in writing from the Publisher.

Bradbury Press
An Affiliate of Macmillan, Inc.
866 Third Avenue, New York, NY 10022
Collier Macmillan Canada, Inc.
Printed and bound in the United States of America
First Edition
10 9 8 7 6 5 4 3 2 1

The text of this book is set in 12 point Times Roman.
Book design by Julie Quan

LIBRARY OF CONGRESS CATALOGING-IN-PUBLICATION DATA
Skurzynski, Gloria.
Dangerous ground / Gloria Skurzynski.—1st ed.
p.   cm.
Summary: While taking one last driving tour of Wyoming
before moving out of state, eleven-year-old Angela
accompanies her beloved seventy-eight-year-old great-aunt Hil
to Yellowstone National Park, where Hil's strange behavior
suggests she may be losing her sanity.
ISBN 0-02-782731-3
[1. Old age—Fiction. 2. Great-aunts—Fiction.
3. Wyoming—Fiction. 4. Yellowstone National
Park—Fiction.] I. Title. PZ7.S6287Dan 1989
[Fic]—dc19 88-31394 CIP AC

To Hilda McCawley, my past, and
Kristin Ferguson, my future, with love

The author wishes to express her thanks to Gary
Brown, Assistant Chief Ranger; Sandi Fowler, Park
Ranger/Bear Management Coordinator; Diane
Fraser-Herring, Park Ranger in Bear Management;
Mary Anne Davis, Librarian in the Yellowstone
Research Library; Emily Anderson, Public Affairs
Office; and Greg Kroll, Special Assistant to the
Superintendent, all with the National Park Service in
Yellowstone National Park.

Contents

1
Playground

"I can't help it," Angela said. "I'm just a kid. I have to do what they tell me."

Angela's words were lost in Sara's wails. "After all the plans we made! Now I'll have to go to seventh grade by myself. How can you desert me like this?"

Angela curled her fingers around the tricky bars. Although patches of snow still lay gray and crusted in the shadow of the school building, May sunshine made the metal bars warm to the touch. "I don't have any choice," she answered. "When my mom and dad called on Sunday—"

"Sunday! This is Thursday. Why did you wait so long to tell me?"

As Angela moved closer to Sara so no one else would hear, wind blew strands of her long blond hair across Sara's dark curls. "I knew how bad you were already feeling," Angela answered softly. "About your grandmother. I didn't want to make you feel worse." The week before, Sara's grandmother had

1

been placed in an old folks' home for her own protection. A victim of Alzheimer's disease, she'd become too confused to live alone.

"Right! First my grandmother gets put away, and now my best friend's moving to a different state!" Sara cried, not caring if everyone on the playground heard her. "I can't stand it! I just cannot stand it!" She wove both arms through the overhead gym bars and hung from them, sagging with dejection. Big tears fell to splotch her blue blouse.

Since only five minutes of recess remained, the tempo and intensity of the games on the playground picked up, along with the noise. A few younger kids looked at Sara, curious, but the older ones were too involved in volleyball, jump rope, or four square to pay much attention to her. Anyway, everyone was used to Sara's tears. She cried often and easily.

Angela didn't cry, not then and not earlier. Not once since her parents telephoned on Sunday had she cried. At night a few small whispers would escape into her pillow: "It'll be okay. I'll be okay." But no tears.

"We were supposed to go to junior high together next year," Sara mourned. "Now what am I going to do?" They'd promised to give each other courage the following September in the big new school, where seventh graders were considered the lowest form of life.

"You'll know lots of other kids," Angela said. "It'll be easier for you than for me. I'll be in a new school, a new city, and a whole new state." And in a new house. Angela and her parents had never before lived all together in a house.

Since she'd started first grade, she'd stayed with her Great-Aunt Hilda McMullen in Casper, Wyoming, from the beginning to the end of each school year. Angela's parents were oil field workers. They traveled all over the Southwest: Texas to Oklahoma to Mexico and everywhere in between where oil wells needed to be drilled. During the summers Angela moved with them from job to job, from motel to motel in city after city. But from September to June, she stayed put in Casper, Wyoming. Or she had, until now.

"Why? Why are your parents taking you away after all these years?" Sara demanded.

"Because they're going to have a baby."

"What!"

"A baby."

"Wow!" The single syllable got drawn out to last a full five seconds. Sara's lips were as round as her eyes, which had stopped squeezing out fresh tears. She grinned. "That's neat!"

"Yeah. Neat," Angela answered. Finger by finger, she pinched the skin on her knuckles into little peaks that flattened almost as soon as she let them go.

Still grinning, Sara told her, "Now you'll get stuck baby-sitting all the time, like I do with my bummy little brother."

"No, I won't."

"Ha! Just wait. You'll see."

"I won't!" Repeating what her father had told her over the phone, Angela said, "My mother will take care of it. She's quitting her job because she wants to stay home with the baby. She says . . . " Her voice cracked slightly, but Sara was too interested in the words to notice. "She says she missed too much of my life, and she's not going to make the same mistake twice."

"That's not fair," Sara said. "If they didn't stay home with you, they shouldn't do it for the new baby, either."

"Sara, that's really dumb."

"It is not. They even bought a house for the new baby, and they never bought a house for you. Where did you say it is? The house?"

"El Paso, Texas." A soccer ball rolled toward them and Angela kicked it back.

"Wow!" Sara said again. "I met a kid from Texas once. He talked funny. If they all talk like that down there, they'll know right away you're a new kid because you'll sound different." The tears were gone—Sara stared at Angela as though she'd already become a little bit alien, which made her more interesting. It wasn't unusual for Sara to blubber one min-

4

ute and bubble the next. Her emotions looped like a roller coaster, while Angela's stayed as steady as a freight train. Still, they got along fine, most of the time.

"Did you tell anyone else?" Sara asked.

"No. I told you first."

"Can I tell everybody?" she begged. "Staci and Heather and Krystal and Jeffrey and Zachary . . . ?"

"Sure, if you want to. Go ahead."

The bell rang then, and Sara raced away to break the news, grabbing the retreating sixth graders before they had a chance to reach the school door.

Angela let go of the tricky bars and scuffed back to class alone.

2
Ant Hil

Angela had on her jeans, so it was all right to sit on the blacktop and lean against the school wall. Since they were her pink Guess? jeans, which matched her jacket, she put her math notebook underneath her for protection.

About once a month her parents sent her something nice to wear. Tucked in with the jeans, or jacket, or skirt, or shirt would be a note that said, "We saw this in a big Dallas department store and it reminded us of you." (Or Tulsa department store, or Albuquerque, Houston, Mexico City, or New Orleans.) No one else in her school had clothes from as many places as Angela had.

School had let out a few minutes earlier that Wednesday, almost a week after she'd told Sara about the move. When the last bell rang, the kids had scooted away like minnows fleeing a rock thrown into a pond. Only a few stragglers still walked past. Some of them called, "Hi, Angela. We'll miss you." One said, "Good-bye, Angela, in case I don't see you again before you move away."

Spreading her fingers, she counted the number of days left until the end of school: Thursday and Friday of this week, then came Memorial Day weekend, which meant no school on Monday, which left only four days next week. After that it would all be over. Her parents would come to pick her up. Good-bye, Wyoming. Next stop, Texas.

The asphalt pavement beneath her had cracks in it, some broad, some hardly wider than a shoestring. In spite of the hundreds of sneakered feet that ran across the blacktop every day, the warm weather had brought thin blades of grass up through the cracks. Lightly, Angela swept her fingers over the tips of the new grass. They were too fine and delicate to even tickle.

She pinched her knuckles, a habit she had when she wanted to push bad thoughts out of her mind. Lots of bad thoughts were trying to crowd in. The day before, she'd gone with Sara to visit Sara's grandmother in the nursing home. That wasn't just bad, it was awful. The sick old woman had stared vacantly at the two girls, and once she'd tried to pluck the flower printed on Angela's blouse. Angela had leaped backward from the clawlike fingers, but Sara had grabbed her grandmother's hand and held it tightly. Then she'd cried.

Sara's grandmother was only sixty-nine. That

was nine years younger than Angela's Great-Aunt Hilda, who was seventy-eight. The difference between the two women was remarkable. Half a block away, Hilda McMullen strode toward the school, her steps brisk and firm. When she saw Angela, she shouted, "Hi, Angel!"

"Hi, Ant Hil," Angela answered.

Ant Hil made a little skip, then blew Angela a kiss. Every Wednesday afternoon, Ant Hil came to the school to talk into a tape recorder. Angela's teacher, Mr. Joyce, took oral histories from all the Wyoming old-timers willing to talk to him. And every Wednesday, while they waited for Mr. Joyce, who was always late, Angela and Ant Hil played computer games.

"Guess what!" Ant Hil called now. "Your parents sent you a videotape—it came in the mail. I didn't open it because it was addressed to you. Maybe you want to go home right now to see it. If you don't want to play games today, I'll understand."

"It's okay," Angela said, getting up. "The videotape will still be there when I get home. We'll play till Mr. Joyce comes."

"Good!" Ant Hil exclaimed, looking pleased. "I'm glad, because after you move to Texas, Angel, I won't get to play computer games anymore."

"Sure you will. Mr. Joyce will let you use the computers as much as you want."

"But it won't be any fun to do it alone." Ant Hil

looked sad for a moment. Then she tossed her head and said, "We won't worry about that. Our last days together are going to be happy. Let's go in and fight the battle of the joysticks."

Sitting in front of the computer screen, Angela wrapped her feet around the legs of the chair and concentrated. She was playing really well. As her score climbed, she jerked the joystick and pressed the red button. The little man on the screen jumped to the right, out of the path of a vampire bat.

That got her to level six! Through five earlier levels she'd jumped her men past speeding bullets, bombs, and space creatures. One after the other, they'd been knocked off girders and ladders to fall head over heels to the bottom of the screen. Now she was on the highest level she'd ever reached, but she had only one man left.

She glanced at the corner of the screen to check her score. That was a mistake. In the split second her concentration wavered, a flying saucer zapped her last man. Pitching forward, he tumbled down to hit his head on the bottom and lie there dead.

"Ten thousand and fifty!" Ant Hil exclaimed. "That's excellent, Angel!"

"For me, maybe," Angela answered, "but it's not anywhere near the fifteen thousand you got last week."

"Still, your control is improving. Practice makes perfect." Ant Hil tucked her cotton housedress under her thin legs and scooted closer to the computer. "My turn now."

Angela scraped her chair backward. She probably wouldn't get to play again that afternoon. Ant Hil's nimble fingers were already maneuvering jumpmen up ladders and across girders as the score on the screen flashed higher and higher. Her control was much better than Angela's. She was so dexterous she could even play with one hand. With her left hand, she fumbled in the pocket of her dress to take out a little bottle of nasal spray and some tissue. She managed to uncap the bottle, sniff the spray, cap it again, and put it back in her pocket, all the while working the joystick with only her right hand.

"Fourteen thousand, nine hundred and seventy-five points," she announced when GAME OVER flashed on the screen. "Fiddle faddle! I wanted to break fifteen thousand like I did last week. It's your turn again, Angel."

"Too late. Here comes Mr. Joyce."

The social studies teacher had just walked into the computer room. "Good afternoon, ladies. Isn't it a glorious May afternoon outside?" he asked.

"Yes and no," Ant Hil answered. "All the trees are in pollen, and that makes me sniff and sneeze. If I didn't have my nasal spray and allergy pills to keep from—"

"Fine, fine," Mr. Joyce answered absently. He plugged in his tape recorder and spoke at it: "Testing,

testing. One, two, three." Satisfied, he said, "Sorry I'm late again, Miss Hilda. One of my students had to stay after school for a makeup test."

"Oh, I don't mind waiting at all. Angel and I have a wonderful time playing with the computer. They never had any gadgets like this when I was a girl."

"I've seen you play," Mr. Joyce said. "You have remarkable dexterity for an ol . . . I mean. . . ."

"You can say it—I'm an old lady. But in my younger days, I was the fastest telegraph operator in the whole state of Wyoming."

"Tell him what they called you, Ant Hil," Angela prompted.

"The other telegraphers called me 'the girl with lightning fingers.'" She held up her hands, which were not at all gnarly and knobby-knuckled like most old folks' hands.

"Speaking of what people call you, Miss Hilda," he said, "I've been meaning to ask about Angela's name for you. Ant Hil. That's kind of unusual, even for a pet name. You know, it sounds like . . . "

"Like an anthill," Ant Hil agreed. "When she was a tiny tyke, 'Great-Aunt Hilda' was too much of a mouthful, so she shortened it. And I call her Angel because that's what she is."

Angela always blushed when Ant Hil said that in front of people. "Do you want me to wait here until you're finished recording?" she asked.

"No, go on home without me. I know you want to see that videotape your parents sent." As Angela started for the door, Ant Hil called after her, "Oh, and don't forget to kill a chicken for supper."

Angela froze.

"Miss Hilda, do you keep chickens?" Mr. Joyce asked. "I didn't think people were allowed to keep chickens inside the Casper city limits."

"We don't have any chickens," Angela said through stiff lips.

"We don't?" Ant Hil frowned. "I thought we did. We used to, didn't we?"

"She's only joking," Angela muttered. Her cheeks burned, but Mr. Joyce wasn't looking at her.

He moved the tape recorder closer to Ant Hil and said, "Well, let's get on with the recording. Now, last week you recalled September of 1930, when the railroad trackmen were ready to go on strike."

Ant Hil's frown smoothed away. "That's right. I remember it as if it happened only yesterday. The union organizers had come to Casper. . . ." She was off once more into the past, and Mr. Joyce pushed buttons to capture it all on tape. "It was a clear and shiny morning—the thermometer on the train station said seventy-three degrees, so I didn't even have on a sweater, just my green lisle blouse and a print skirt. Around the bend, the workers came into sight, marching right on the railroad tracks, you see, so that if the trains kept moving, they'd run down the strikers." Her voice rose with excitement as she recalled, "I stood at the window with my fingers on the telegraph key, ready to wire for medical help, because if those trains didn't stop in time . . ."

Quietly, Angela left them. Outside, she pulled her pink jacket tightly around her, even though sunshine warmed the schoolyard. Chickens! Whatever had made Ant Hil think of chickens?

She slipped around the side of the school to peer through a window into the computer room. There sat Ant Hil, seeming perfectly normal, telling Mr. Joyce every detail of a union strike that had happened sixty years ago. Right after she'd told Angela to kill a chicken that didn't exist!

It was the third time that week Ant Hil had said something really weird. Angela shuddered, thinking of Sara's grandmother.

3

Angela

Sara had said her grandmother's mind was gone. Where did a mind go when it went, Angela wondered as she let herself through the front door of her home. How did it start to go? Just a little at a time? Did it begin the journey with small slips, like a question about imaginary chickens? She closed the front door, trying to shut all her worries on the other side of it.

On the hall table lay the package from her parents. Every now and then they sent Angela a videotape to show her where they were and what they'd been doing. She could always recognize a videotape— the package was a certain shape and it rattled when she shook it. This one was postmarked El Paso, Texas. On the brown paper wrapping her mother had written, in purple fine-line pen, TO: Miss Angela Anderson.

Slowly, because there was no one else in the house to hurry her, she unwrapped the package. A hastily scrawled Post-it note in her father's handwrit-

14

ing was stuck to the sleeve of the videotape. It said, "Here's something you'll want to see from two people who love you. There's a message for Aunt Hilda in the tape, too."

After she slipped the tape into the VCR, Angela kicked off her shoes and leaned against a pile of pillows on the sofa. The television screen turned blue with Texas sky. High on the top of an oil derrick, a man in a yellow hard hat waved to her. It was her father. Her mother must have been operating the video camcorder.

The next shot was a closer one of her father, at the bottom of the derrick. Like a trapeze performer, he stood on a section of drill pipe that swung from a chain as it moved toward the shaft. The coat of mud on his boots reached all the way up to cover the knees of his Levis; his shirt and Levi jacket, too, were stained with mud and grease. Oil drillers called their work clothes "greasers" for a good reason.

Angela admired her tall, husky father, whose sure moves showed that he knew what he was doing. He guided the drill stem into another section of pipe, then tightened it with a wrench huge enough for the Jolly Green Giant. Grease oozed out between the tight joints. When that was done, he took a step backward on the platform.

"Hi, Angela," he said. "Here's where we're working this week. I hope we're lucky and strike oil this time—the last two jobs turned out to be dry holes. Mom's taking this video not just for you, but for me too, as a souvenir, because this is my last job out on the oil patch."

Next she saw a close-up of her father's smiling face. It was speckled with grease. Flecks of grease clung to his thick blond mustache; he wiped it with a gloved hand before he said, "Yep, this is the end for your old dad. No more oil field gypsy. From now on I'm going to work in the corporate office in El Paso while Mom stays home to bake pies and stuff. Right, Mom?" When he grinned, his teeth looked extra white against his tanned, ruddy skin.

Then the camera seemed to move away so the whole drill rig showed on the screen, all the way to the top of the derrick. Her father and three other crewmen waved right at Angela, although actually they would have been waving at her mother, who was doing the filming. Or maybe they were waving good-bye to her father, since he was leaving his dangerous job as a wildcat oil driller.

Her mother's job was just as exciting. Since most wildcat drilling took place out on ranches, Angela's mother had to make all the arrangements with the ranchers before the drill rigs arrived. She got leases signed, located water, and figured out the best routes, over three or four thousand acres of ranch land, for the huge drill rigs to cross. Then, after the drilling was finished, she took care of the bills for damage to the land. Sometimes her job became dangerous, too—if a rancher thought he'd been cheated, he might lie in wait for the crew with a shotgun.

The television scene changed. Angela's father evidently was operating the camcorder now, because her mother appeared on the screen. "Here it is, Angela," she said. "Our new house in El Paso."

It was pretty, with white frame on top and red brick on the bottom, but Angela didn't look at the rooms her mother was showing proudly, one by one. She was much more intrigued by her mother's new shape. Kneeling in front of the TV, she touched the screen, touched the bulge that showed under her mother's maternity top. That was where the baby grew.

Then her mother turned so the bulge didn't show. "This will be your room, Angela," she said. "From the window, you can see the Rio Grande. We'll paint it any shade you want. The room, not the river." She giggled. "You can pick out the furniture and do all your own decorating. Do you like it?"

Angela didn't know. It was hard to decide about a bedroom squeezed onto a nineteen-inch screen.

They must have put the camcorder onto a tripod then, because both her parents came into view at the same time. "This room is for you, Aunt Hilda," they said, and swept their arms wide to show a bright room with French windows and hardwood floors. "We want you to live with us—"

Angela stopped the tape. Watching Ant Hil's

part of it would be like reading Ant Hil's mail before she opened it. Still on her knees, she rewound the tape and turned the volume all the way off. The picture came on the screen again, but this time there was no sound.

When her father appeared, waving from the top of the derrick, Angela said, "Dad, I've got to talk to you. To you and Mom. There's no one else for me to talk to." With a catch in her voice she said, "Something's wrong with Ant Hil. I think maybe she's getting Alzheimer's disease, like Sara's grandma has."

Her father stepped backward on the drill platform.

"The first time I noticed, we were in the yard looking at the crocuses. Ant Hil said, 'Crocuses are your favorite flower, Margaret.' I said, 'You called me Margaret, Ant Hil. I'm not Margaret.' And, Dad, she looked straight at me and said, 'Of course you're Margaret. You're my baby sister.' "

Angela put both hands on the television screen to touch her father's smiling face. "She wasn't teasing, Dad, I swear. She really thought I was her sister Margaret. It only lasted a minute, but it scared me."

Her mother climbed the steps to the front porch of the new house and Angela leaned her forehead onto the screen. "Oh, Mom, I wish you were here right now. Help me! I don't know what to do! The next time Ant Hil said something crazy, we were in the beauty shop. I was getting my bangs cut. All of

18

a sudden she looked in the mirror and said, 'My hair is gray!' Like it had just turned gray that minute. She seemed so surprised, Mom, and she wasn't faking it. 'When did it turn gray?' she asked me. I didn't know what to say."

Angela looked longingly at both parents, who stood smiling with their arms around one another. She hadn't been with them since Christmas, and more than anything she wanted them to hold her, to hug her.

"Then today, when she started to tape record for Mr. Joyce—"

The front door opened. "I'm home, Angel," Ant Hil called out. "Are you looking at the tape your parents sent?"

"Yes, but this next part is for you. I didn't want to watch it until you got here." Pretending she'd only been adjusting the volume, Angela turned it up and moved back onto the sofa. Ant Hil sat down beside her.

The old woman watched in silence as Angela's parents begged her to come live in El Paso. No more harsh Wyoming winters, they said. Aunt Hilda was growing too old to fight snow and ice every year. They'd be one big happy family together. The house had four bedrooms—a separate room for everyone, except, of course, Angela's parents, who would share the master bedroom. Just look at these flowers, they said, and the screen filled with close-ups of nasturtiums and geraniums and marigolds. That's how it is in El Paso in May, they said. In Wyoming, they bet, the forsythia wouldn't even be out yet.

Ant Hil stayed silent when the tape ended and the television set buzzed with static. Angela turned it off and asked, "Well?"

"Well, what?"

"Will you come to live in El Paso?"

Her gray head shook in gentle refusal. "I was born in Wyoming, and I plan to stay here to die in Wyoming, whenever that should happen."

"Ant Hil!"

"Angel, look around you." Ant Hil got up and moved slowly through the room. "This mirror belonged to my mother. She had it shipped here from the East. I remember the day the delivery man brought it in his horse-drawn wagon. It was packed in straw, and after he hung the mirror on the wall, he let me feed the straw to his horse."

Softly, she touched the piano keys. "My little sister Margaret, who was your grandmother, practiced in this room every day after school. She was so good, Angel! I thought she might become a concert pianist, but she met your grandfather and got married."

Angela told her, "You can bring all these things to El Paso with you."

"I couldn't. They wouldn't go with your parents' new, modern house. They'd be out of place, and so would I. The old can't live with the young."

"Sure they can. You and I have been living together for six years, and we get along great," Angela argued.

"That's because you're *very* young and I'm *very* old. Put another generation in between us, and there'd be trouble. Anyway, I don't want to leave here. This house is filled with all my memories." She went to the hall and raised the curtain. "I can look into the yard and see the lilac bush I planted forty years ago. Behind the bush, way in the back, there used to be a chicken coop. When I was little, I gathered eggs every day."

"You don't have to make up your mind right now," Angela pleaded. She almost stumbled when she used the word "mind." If Ant Hil's mind really was going, she'd need someone to look after her, and she had no more family left in Casper.

"Let's not talk about it," Ant Hil said. "Let's just be happy. Remember, we're having a big Thanksgiving celebration the day after tomorrow."

4
Scrabble

In her last growth spurt, Angela had caught up to Ant Hil's height. Sixty-one inches. They weighed almost the same, too—eighty-seven pounds for Angela to ninety-two for Ant Hil. That made Angela an average-sized kid while Ant Hil was small and wiry for an old woman.

Her size didn't stop Ant Hil from single-handedly wrestling a big turkey out of the roasting pan. "Done to a turn," she said, and sniffed approvingly. "Thanksgiving in May."

It had been Ant Hil's idea to celebrate Thanksgiving early, on Memorial Day weekend. "You won't be here next November," she told Angela, "and heaven knows what people eat for Thanksgiving in Texas. Chili, probably. To be safe, we'll have your turkey dinner here. You can invite Sara to eat with us and sleep over."

It was Friday when they celebrated, but that didn't matter, Ant Hil said. At the dinner table she

22

told Sara and Angela, "The earliest Thanksgivings were on lots of different days of the week. Having it the last Thursday of November didn't start until 1863, when Lincoln was president."

Impressed, Sara asked, "How do you remember things like that, Miss Hilda?"

"Abraham Lincoln is my favorite president," Ant Hil answered. "I learned about his Thanksgiving proclamation when I was a schoolgirl, like you."

Everything about the dinner was perfect. The turkey, waiting on its big wooden platter for Ant Hil's carving knife, looked like an illustration from a cookbook. In the center of the table, a crystal bowl held a dozen fat, purple lilacs. "I brought them inside two days ago so they'd open up all the way for to-night," Ant Hil mentioned. "How often can people enjoy fresh lilacs for Thanksgiving?"

"I thought they made you sneeze," Angela said.

"They do, but I just took two allergy pills, so that should keep me for a while."

Sara said, "The table looks beautiful, Miss Hilda. My mother could never use a lace cloth like this because my little brother would wipe his grubby hands on it."

"Ant Hil always uses lace," Angela told her. When she was small, she would crawl under the table to pretend it was a secret cave. No one else could enter, because in Angela's imagination, the hanging tablecloth became a magical spider web that kept bad

23

things away. She no longer remembered what dangers it was supposed to protect her from, but she remembered how safe she felt there, surrounded by webs of lace.

"More turkey? More stuffing? Eat up!" Ant Hil urged them.

They ate and talked and lingered over the feast until the candlewicks burned long and they had no more room for even a spoonful of whipped cream. "Let's play Scrabble," Sara suggested then. "I never get to play it at home. We only do games like Candy Land so my brother can play, too. And he cheats all the time."

"Sara, he's only three," Angela said.

"So? It's no fun to play dumb baby games with a cheater. That's why I like to play Scrabble when I come here."

"All right. I'll get rid of these dishes in a hurry," Ant Hil said. "You girls set up the card table in the living room."

Ant Hil was a much better speller than either Angela or Sara. Each time they played Scrabble, she challenged them on every suspicious word they tried to slip onto the board. Whenever they looked up the word in the dictionary, Ant Hil always turned out to be right. As usual, she won the first game easily that evening.

After the second game she mentioned, "I bought

some cider at the supermarket. That's part of Thanksgiving, too. Shall we have it now?"

"I'll get it," Angela said. "I want to open a window anyway." The house felt so warm it was making her sleepy. Big Thanksgiving dinners belonged with cold weather and snow, not with May evenings when lilacs smelled sweet on the dining room table.

As she pushed through the swinging door to the kitchen, she felt a blast of hot air that made her reel backward. All four burners on the gas range had been turned on to the highest heat. How could that have happened? Maybe Ant Hil had been trying to burn off spills or something, but it looked like an inferno. The blue flames jetted upward, wavering a little in the draft from the door, radiating heat waves toward the ceiling. Angela twisted the knobs to shut off the gas, then threw open the kitchen window and flapped a dish towel to clear away the hot air.

The bottle of cider waited on the counter, but she couldn't find any glasses. They're probably in the dishwasher, she thought. When she opened it, the dishwasher was empty.

"This is getting weirder and weirder," she muttered. "What happened to the dinner dishes?"

The familiar scared feeling, as if her insides were being squeezed, started small and grew bigger while she searched the kitchen. How could a whole load of dirty dishes disappear? On a hunch, she opened the oven, and her fear turned to dismay.

The unwashed supper dishes had been stacked neatly inside the oven. Knives and forks, the gravy bowl, the cut-glass pitcher that once belonged to Angela's grandmother—all were carefully arranged on the oven racks. Ant Hil must have mistaken the oven for the dishwasher. She'd loaded it, and then turned it on. Only what she'd really turned on were the burners on top of the stove.

From the living room Ant Hil called, "What's taking you so long, Angel? Where's the cider?"

"In a minute!"

She stood there staring into the oven. Three times now Ant Hil had said weird things, but this was the first time she'd ever *done* anything strange. Worse than strange, it was dangerous! It could have caused a fire. Angela had an awful image of flames creeping up the kitchen curtains, jumping to devour the painted yellow daisies on the kitchen cabinets, roaring through the rest of the house. She pinched the skin on her knuckles so hard her breath caught from the pain.

Should she make Ant Hil come into the kitchen and look at what she'd done?

No, Sara was there. If she called Ant Hil, Sara would come too, and would find out that Ant Hil was acting odd. "In a minute," she yelled again. Quickly, she took the dishes out of the oven, piled them into the dishwasher, and turned it on.

"There weren't enough clean glasses," she said when she went back into the living room. "I guess you forgot to start the dishwasher, Ant Hil. Don't worry, I did it."

"Oh, my memory!" As though to give her memory a little push, Ant Hil brushed a hand through the short gray hair that fluffed around her forehead. "It's getting worse all the time. I'd forget my head if it weren't fastened on. Sit down and play, Angel. Sara and I started another game while you were in the kitchen, and it's your turn."

She glanced at the letters they'd drawn for her. Only one vowel, and the rest consonants. *J, Y, Z, L, R, C,* and an *A*. Although she was too worried to care about a silly game, a word leaped right out at her from those seven Scrabble tiles. *C-R-A-Z-Y*.

After a moment she placed *J-A-R* on the board, connecting it to an *S* already there.

"*Jars.* That's eleven points, but the *J* was on a double letter score so it goes up to eighteen, Angel," Ant Hil announced. She marked it on the score pad.

How could anyone add that fast and yet stack dirty dishes in an oven? Through lowered eyelids, Angela studied her great-aunt. She was laughing at something she'd just seen on television—she could watch television and at the same time arrange Scrabble tiles with those lightning fingers, fingers that had once tapped out swift messages over railroad telegraph wires.

"There!" she said. *"Phoenix.* Now don't you girls challenge me by saying that's a proper name. I know it's the name of a city in Arizona, but it's also a mythical bird, so I can use it. That's nineteen points for me, plus a triple-letter score for the *X,* which makes it thirty-five. Your turn, Sara."

"Okay." Sara picked up the tiles, arranged them alphabetically, and settled her round chin onto her fists. She always took ages to decide on a word.

On the television, a news program started. "Alzheimer's disease," the commentator said, "now affects up to fifteen percent of all Americans over the age of sixty-five. That's one in every seven."

One in seven! Angela sat up straight.

"Is *ruggle* a word?" Sara asked.

"If you put it down, I'll challenge you," Ant Hil told her.

"Slowly, relentlessly," the newscaster continued, "Alzheimer's disease destroys brain cells. It can begin with a slight loss of memory. The victim might forget a phone number or a friend's name. Other common symptoms are hallucinations and strange behavior."

"How about *gluer?* You know—a person who glues something," Sara explained, deliberately ignoring the television report. From painful personal experience, Sara already knew more about Alzheimer's than she wanted to. "They'd be called a gluer, wouldn't they?"

Ant Hil nodded. "I won't challenge that."

Carefully, Sara spelled *gluer* on the board. "Your turn," she told Angela.

Angela didn't hear. She was staring intently at the television, where a middle-aged woman said to a white-haired man, "No, Dad, don't put the fork in your glass. Use it to eat the food on your plate." Puzzled, the old man picked up a carrot with his fingers.

"Angel, your turn," Ant Hil repeated.

"Huh? Oh!" Angela quickly took a *D* and an *O* from her rack. She joined them to the *G* on Sara's *gluer* to make *dog*.

"You won't get many points for a little word like that," Sara said.

Angela didn't care. On television, a thin woman was saying, "It's funny, Mother can remember things from the past, like the words to an old song, but usually she can't remember my name."

Angela jumped up from her chair.

"Why did you turn off the TV?" Ant Hil asked.

"It was just a dumb news program. Why is it there's never anything good on on Friday nights? If we're going to play Scrabble, let's play Scrabble!" She sat back down and checked the score pad. Angela 41, Sara 73, Hilda 126.

There couldn't be anything wrong with Ant Hill! Everyone forgot things sometimes, or did something strange. Why once, Angela remembered, she'd put her geography book in the clothes hamper by mistake, and couldn't find it for a week. Even kids did stupid things.

"Whose turn is it?" she asked. "Let's play!"

5
Sleepover

"After I finish braiding your hair," Sara announced, "I'm going to put on some press-on nails. I brought a new bottle of nail polish. Wait till you see the color!" She sat on the edge of Angela's bed while Angela sat on the floor, leaning against the bed. "It's called 'Crimson Claws.'"

It was lucky Sara hadn't put on the press-on nails before she started fooling with Angela's hair, or they might have gouged her scalp. As it was, Sara's comb and fingers felt soothing. Angela leaned back, enjoying the pleasant touch, and said, "Could I ask you something, Sara?"

"Sure."

"When your grandmother first started getting Alzheimer's disease, how did she act? I mean, what did she do at first that made you wonder—"

"I don't want to talk about it," Sara said. "Why do you want to know such awful stuff? If I talk about it I'll just start to cry, and it will spoil our sleepover.

This is probably the last one we'll ever have." Sara's voice had already begun to quaver.

"You're right," Angela said. "I shouldn't have asked. I'm sorry."

Unpredictable as usual, Sara relented. "Well, if you really want to know . . . first Grandma just forgot everything, like what day it was, and where the bathroom was, and things like that. She'd go out for walks and she couldn't find her way home. Why are you asking me this?"

Angela tried to keep her face smooth and unconcerned. Digging for information was risky. Sara was no dummy; she might figure out where the questions were leading, and if Sara probed a little, if she pushed the right buttons, Angela might break down and spill out all the strange things Ant Hil had recently said and done. She didn't want to do that. "Never discuss family troubles with people outside the family," Ant Hil always advised. "Long after you've forgotten what you said, the outsiders will remember."

Angela would be able to talk to her parents on Sunday—they telephoned every weekend to find out whether things were going all right. Or she might even wait until they came to take her to Texas. By that time, if Ant Hil had stopped acting strange, the problem would have solved itself and Angela wouldn't have to say anything to anyone. Better wait, she decided.

She smiled up at Sara. "It was dumb of me to

bring it up about your grandmother. What I really wanted to know was—what's it like to live with your mom and dad and brother all in the same house?"

Sara pulled the brush through Angela's long hair twice before she answered. "It's nice sometimes and yucky sometimes—about even. You know, just a normal family."

Normal. Angela had never experienced normal family life. "If it's about even between nice and yucky, why are you always complaining about your little brother?" she asked.

"Well, I really love him when he's sweet, and he's sweet a lot of the time. I complain because I have to baby-sit him so much." Sara's fingers moved surely, separating Angela's hair into strands. "At least my brother is toilet-trained. *You* will have to change smelly diapers. You say you won't have to baby-sit, but just wait till your mother runs out of groceries or something. It'll be like this. . . ." Sara mimicked, " 'Angela, would you mind the baby for a few minutes while I run to the store? Oh, and I have to stop at the post office—I need some stamps. But I won't be long.' " In her own voice, Sara added, "And the few minutes always turns into at least an hour. So then you have to feed him, too, and change his diaper. In fact, about two minutes after your mother leaves the house, I promise you the baby will mess his diaper a big one. That's life, Angela."

Angela slumped against the bed. She knew nothing about diaper-changing, or about babies, either. If Sara had had a baby sister three years ago, instead of a baby brother, Angela might have volunteered to change a diaper once in a while. But changing a boy baby had seemed too complicated.

"What'll we do now?" Sara asked. "I'm finished with your hair." She'd braided Angela's thick, long, blond hair only at the crown, twisted the braid into a butterfly shape, and fastened it with a barrette that had a butterfly on it. Angela stood up to look at herself in the mirror. She liked the effect.

"I know what we'll do," Sara said, answering her own question. "We'll make a list."

"What kind of list?"

"A list of things we want in a best friend. You know, both of us will need new best friends when school starts in September. I've been trying to decide between Staci and Heather and Krystal—"

Hurt, Angela broke in, "Couldn't you at least wait till I'm gone? I'll only be here one more week. It's like you're burying me before I'm dead!"

Sara got up to put away the comb and brush, but Angela could see that she was blushing. When she turned back she said in a meek voice, "Sorry. It's just . . . I'm not like you, Angela. You can handle everything by yourself. Me, I'm scared. I need someone."

Angela sighed. "Okay. Get the pencil and notebook from my desk."

Sara sat back down on the floor, then riffled through the notebook to a clean page. "Now, what's the most important thing about a best friend?" she asked. "First, she shouldn't be rude and she shouldn't be snobby."

"That's not what she should be, it's what she shouldn't be."

"Right." Sara was busy writing. "So you make up the next ones."

Angela traced her finger across the ridges and valleys where threads quilted her bedspread. "Best friends shouldn't always ask to borrow your homework."

"That leaves out Krystal," Sara said. "Here's another shouldn't—a best friend shouldn't always talk about what things cost. Like, you know Staci? She always says, 'These shoes are real leather, and they cost fifty dollars.' You never say things like that, Angela, and I know some of your clothes cost a lot. So if I cross out Krystal and Staci . . ."

Rising onto her knees, Angela asked, "Why does a best friend have to be a girl?"

Sara looked startled. "You wouldn't want a *boy* for a best friend!"

"I like lots of boys as friends."

"Yeah, but not as *best* friends. You could never talk to them about personal stuff," Sara said. "It would be too embarrassing, and they might go out and tell other boys what you said."

"True. A best friend needs to listen a lot and not blab everything you say."

"That lets out Heather," Sara said. She put down the notebook. "She never listens because she's always talking. Not like you, Angela. You're a great listener. You just never talk."

Surprised, Angela got up to sit on the edge of the bed and stare in puzzlement at Sara. "What do you mean? I talk to you all the time."

"Sure you do, about things like school, and TV, and which boys you like, and which ones are really rude. But you never talk about important stuff, like how you feel about the baby your mother's going to have. Krystal says you're as secret as the FBI."

"You were talking about me to Krystal?"

Sara ducked her head and looked guilty. "Don't hate me. It's like I've been . . . interviewing different girls. Junior high starts in September, so I only have three months to find a new friend." Tears came to Sara's eyes. "It isn't easy, Angela. No one else is as nice as you."

A soft knock sounded on the door. "It's midnight, girls," Ant Hil said through the door. "Please turn out the light now and stop talking."

"Okay," they answered together.

In silence, in the darkness, they slid into the sleeping bags on the floor. Neither of them would use the bed that night, since it wouldn't be fair for one to get the bed. Holding hands, they whispered about how they'd miss each other, and Sara cried a little more. Her last words, in a blurred, sleepy whisper, were, "We never got to do the press-on nails and the 'Crimson Claws.'" Then her hand went limp.

How could Sara be sad and still fall asleep so quickly? Angela wondered. She felt too hot, so she put one leg out of the sleeping bag, but her foot felt cold then so she put it back in again. With her hands behind her head, she lay staring at the pale pattern the streetlight made on the ceiling, wanting to fall asleep fast like Sara, but knowing she wouldn't. Too much was worrying her.

The door to her bedroom cracked open. Gliding like a ghost in her long flannel nightgown, Ant Hil drifted over to Angela's sleeping bag. Angela pretended to be asleep, but she could hear Ant Hil's puff of breath as the old woman knelt down beside her. Fingertips lighter than a butterfly's wings swept Angela's cheek, making her eyelashes flutter, but in the dark, Ant Hil couldn't see that. Rising after a moment, she left the room as silently as she'd entered.

Lately she'd been doing that a lot. Almost every night since they'd learned Angela was leaving, Ant Hil had come into her room. If she saw that Angela was awake, she would make some excuse, like "I just wanted to close your window, Angel, in case it rains." Or, "Do you need another blanket? It might get chilly."

When Angela replied that she was fine, Ant Hil

would wag her fingers in a little wave from the door, and say, "Well, good-night, then. Sleep well. I'll see you in the morning."

Watching the tree shadows quiver across the windowpane like Ant Hil's waving fingers, Angela listened to the wind. In Wyoming, even in springtime, the wind blew all the time. Sometimes it sounded lonely, whistling soft and low. Other times it blew harder and crept up and down the scale, like the music in a horror movie. Tonight, the wind moaned, matching her mood.

6
Surprises

Ant Hil was probably the best pancake-maker in all of Casper. On Saturday morning, she happily refilled Angela's and Sara's plates as often as they were emptied. "Here," she kept urging, "have more. You're growing girls."

"I've already grown enough this morning," Sara said, patting her tummy. "Anyway, I have to leave right away. My drill team lesson starts in ten minutes. I'll come back later for my sleeping bag and stuff, okay?"

"Don't bother," Angela told her. "I'll bring it to your house this afternoon." Sara lived only three blocks away.

"Great! I'm baby-sitting this afternoon—when you come, I'll let you practice on my little brother." Sara grinned, but almost immediately her eyes began to mist. "You know, this was our last breakfast together after a sleepover." At the door, she turned to them with tears on her cheeks. "I'll remember this breakfast always, Miss Hilda. Thank you for your hospitality. Angela, it was so wonderful. . . ." She ran out then and slammed the door behind her.

"Hormones," Ant Hil said. "They cause moodiness. I well remember how it used to be, but I could always handle it. Sara's older than you, isn't she, Angel?"

Angela nodded. "Not that much older, though. She was twelve in February and I'll be twelve in August."

"I hope when you reach her stage of development," Ant Hil said, "you don't get as emotional as Sara. Giggling one minute and crying the next."

"I like her just the way she is," Angela said, defending her.

"Well, of course. So do I. Sara's a darling girl, and she's been a good best friend."

Best friend. Angela's best friend wasn't Sara, it was the small woman who stood at the sink scrubbing the griddle with a Brillo pad. She went up behind her and put her arms around Ant Hil's waist. "I don't want to leave you," she said.

"I don't want you to leave me, either. Oh, how much I don't want you to leave me! But Angel, you're going to have a real family now—your mother and dad and a new baby brother or sister. You'll like that, won't you?"

"Why can't we all just live together?" Angela asked.

"Your parents have their life, and I have mine. That's how it has to be." She said it matter-of-factly, but her voice sounded unsteady. "Listen, Angel, why don't you finish cleaning the kitchen while I do some shopping? I'll bring you back a surprise."

Angela groaned. "I don't need a surprise every time I feel bad about something. I'm not six anymore."

"Well, I know that." Ant Hil wiped her hands on a dish towel. "But everyone likes surprises, no matter how old they get. I'll find you something super special."

"Ant Hil, even if you got me the most super surprise in the whole universe, I'd still feel bad about leaving you."

Abruptly, Ant Hil poured a glass of water and carried it into the dining room. Angela followed to find her standing next to the table, pressing her fingertips against her eyelids.

"Darn allergies! Tree pollen doesn't just make me sneeze, it makes my eyes water, too," she said. She shook a pill out of a small box and swallowed it.

The watering in her eyes didn't look like the kind caused by pollen. It looked like old-fashioned tears, but Ant Hil would never let Angela see her cry. Once she'd told Angela, "There's nothing as unappealing as a weepy old woman always feeling sorry for herself. I'll never be like that!"

Now she straightened and said, "Well, Angel, I'm off! See you in a little bit."

"Bye." Angela returned to the kitchen and began to clear the dishes. When she heard the front door close behind Ant Hil, she sank down again and buried her head in her arms.

For six years, except during the summers, she'd sat at that kitchen table for breakfast, across from Ant Hil. She remembered the first time, when she was a very small child, the morning she'd been awakened by the slam of a car door. It was her parents' car; she realized that instantly, and when she heard the motor start, she knew they were leaving her.

Screaming, she'd run down the stairs dragging her limp teddy bear by one arm. At the bottom of the steps, Ant Hil had caught her.

"Let me go!" she'd shrieked, struggling to get loose.

"They didn't want to wake you," Ant Hil explained, holding her tightly. "They thought it would be better not to."

"Mommy! Daddy!" Angela had wailed. "Don't go without me!"

Her parents had tried to prepare her. They'd explained it all to her—that she had to stay in Casper with Ant Hil because it was time to go to school. They'd kept her with them as long as they could, even letting her skip kindergarten to travel with them.

Riding in the car from job to job, and in grubby motel rooms where the sinks had rust stains and the thin mattresses sagged, her parents had taken turns teaching Angela numbers and letters. Soon she could read certain familiar words on road signs, like *sale* and *taco stand* and *best deal in town*.

Then she'd turned six. She had to start first grade, her parents explained, because she needed more teaching than they could provide. It couldn't be put off any longer. So Angela had known what was going to happen, and she'd known why, but nothing could have prepared her for the grief she felt when she heard the car drive away. She'd thrashed in Ant Hil's arms until Ant Hil put her down. Then she'd collapsed on the hall floor to scream her pain, fear, and rage.

"This teddy bear is pathetic," Ant Hil had declared. She'd stooped to pick him up. "How would you like it, Angel, if you only had one eye?"

Angela's fists covered both her eyes, but she spread her fingers just enough to peek at Ant Hil and the bear while she continued to cry.

"I think," Ant Hil said, "that I'll find another eye for this poor bear."

Angela twisted around to watch, but Ant Hil had moved out of her range of vision, so she wailed louder.

Quickly, Ant Hil returned with the bear in one hand and a jar in another. It was a large jar, the kind dill pickles come in. She sank onto the floor beside Angela and opened the jar. "This is my button treasury," she announced.

Angela peeked again. Filled to the top, the jar held buttons of every size and color. As she watched, Ant Hil dug her hands into the buttons and lifted them, letting them fall through her fingers like coins.

"Let's see," she'd said. "What color eye shall we pick? Yellow? If the bear has one yellow eye, he'll be searching for honey all the time."

Angela's sobs slowed to whimpers. She frowned.

"If we give him a blue eye," Ant Hil went on, "he'll just lie on his back and look at the sky all day."

"That's silly," Angela said scornfully.

"Of course," Ant Hil told her, "we could find him a brown eye to match his other one. But he doesn't have to have matching eyes. I once saw a man right here in Casper who had two different-colored eyes. One was as green as a frog, and the other as brown as my shoe."

Angela unwound herself from the tight ball on the floor and sat up. "I don't believe you," she said.

"It's true, I swear." Ant Hil raised her right hand solemnly. "I saw him in the supermarket. Maybe if we drive down to the supermarket right now, we'll see him again."

Angela had shaken her head. "No, we won't. Nobody has two different-colored eyes."

"Well, if he's not there so I can prove it to you," Ant Hil said, "we can buy some chocolate-covered doughnuts for breakfast so the trip won't be wasted. Or some maple bars, or a box of special cereal. You'll have to show me your favorite cereal, Angel."

Slowly, still frowning, Angela had risen to her feet. "If I go, I want a surprise," she demanded.

"Oh, do you like surprises? So do I!" Ant Hil took Angela's hand and began to lead her up the stairs to get dressed. The bear had trailed from Angela's other hand, bumping up a step at a time.

"I promise I'll buy you something special," Ant Hil had said, "but you can't see it till we get home. Otherwise it won't be a surprise, will it?"

For that first month, a surprise waited on Angela's pillow each day when she came home from school. Coloring books, little plastic dolls, erasers shaped like spaceships—nothing expensive, but all of them fun. As Angela grew older, Ant Hil still brought her surprises from time to time. Now they were teenage things, like magazines, or barrettes, or one time, a bottle of Très L.A. cologne.

She stood up to finish clearing the table. In spite of her unhappiness, she smiled a little, wondering what Ant Hil would bring this time.

7

White Ford Truck

A horn honked twice, so loud it had to be coming from their own driveway. Angela put down the teen magazine she was reading and went to the window.

A tall white pickup truck stood parked in the driveway, gleaming as only brand-new vehicles can. In the truck cab, behind the wheel, sat Ant Hil. When she saw Angela peering through the curtain, she waved for her to come out.

"How do you like it?" Ant Hil asked through the driver's window. "Some surprise, huh?"

"Whose is it?" Angela asked. She stood on tiptoe to peer inside.

"It's ours. At least for a while, anyway. I rented it—the Ford dealer here in Casper is an old friend. Isn't it nice?"

Nice! It was fantastic—new and expensive and big. It looked almost too big for Ant Hil to handle.

She turned off the ignition and spoke excitedly

46

in the quiet after the roar. "Look, Angel, it has a camper shell on it. Let's throw a few things into the back and try it out."

"You mean, go for a drive? Now?"

"No time like the present," Ant Hil answered. She opened the door and slid her bottom over the edge of the seat as if it were a sliding board, because she was too short to step down to the driveway. Her sensible brown shoes hit the asphalt with a thump. "I'll grab some things we need while you pack the food. Get the Styrofoam cooler. First empty all the ice-cube trays into it, then put in the leftover turkey from last night and a jar of mustard and—"

"Where are we going?" Angela interrupted.

"Who knows?" Ant Hil threw the truck keys into the air and caught them. "Let's be daring! Let's act a little crazy for a change."

Angela winced.

"Honestly, Angel," she said, trotting to the back door with Angela following, "anyone would think you were the old lady and I was the little girl. Where's your sense of adventure?"

Well, why not? Angela thought. Ant Hil wanted to drive around and picnic along the side of the road. What was wrong with that? "Okay," she said. "I'll pack some bread and cookies and oranges, too."

"That's the spirit!" Ant Hil thumped her on the back. "Let's both hurry and see if we can put everything together in fifteen minutes. Ready? Go!" She bolted across the kitchen. Angela could hear her run up the stairs.

Leaning on the open refrigerator door, Angela stared absently at the half-carved turkey. Was this a normal way for an elderly woman to behave, or was it another of Ant Hil's strangenesses? She seemed perfectly fine, though. Her rapid footsteps continued overhead, in the bedrooms and the hall and the bathroom, accompanied by thumps and thuds as doors opened and banged shut.

"So okay," Angela said to herself, and she began to pull things from the refrigerator. "Might as well do it right." Getting into the mood, she grabbed individually wrapped Swiss cheese slices, a jar of sweet pickles, a six-pack of orange drink, two fat tomatoes, and half-full jars of mayonnaise and mustard. From the silverware drawer she took two each of knives, forks, and spoons, added a paring knife and napkins, pulled the roll of paper towels off the rack, and loaded everything into three supermarket sacks.

Ant Hil had begun to make trips up and down the steps and out the front door, rather than coming through the back door. After the third trip she hurried into the kitchen and stood there, panting and grinning at Angela. She'd changed into slacks and a white sweater with Norwegian designs, and she was wearing her western hat.

"Why the cowboy hat?" Angela asked.

"To get into the spirit of things. If we're going to see Wyoming, I want to look appropriate. I just need to get my allergy pills and our heavy coats and then we can leave," she said.

"Heavy coats? It's warm outside."

"This is Wyoming, remember?" Ant Hil answered. "The wind can start blowing fifty miles an hour in a minute. It could even snow!"

"Ant Hil, it's sixty-two degrees today."

"You never know, in Wyoming. We'll take coats and hats. I'll get them while you load the food into the back of the truck."

Angela carried two sacks the first time. The tailgate had been lowered; she set the food on it while she peered inside to get her first view of the camper shell. Whatever Ant Hil had packed was covered with a blanket. It looked as if she'd brought an awful lot of stuff for a picnic.

When Angela went back for the third sack, she had to squeeze past Ant Hil coming through the back door with her arms full of their heavy coats. "On your way out," Ant Hil said, "make sure the door's locked."

The first thing Angela noticed when she climbed into the truck cab was the wonderful new-car smell. The vinyl bucket seats felt more comfortable than their furniture in the living room. "This is neat!" she exclaimed.

"It certainly is," Ant Hil said, "except they

make these things to fit great big cowboys instead of little old ladies." She'd brought two pillows from her bed, one to sit on and one to lean against. Propped up that way, Ant Hil could see better to drive.

"Seat belts fastened? Then we're off!" she cried, and backed the truck out into the street.

8

Chugwater

"Just look at it," Ant Hil said.

"At what?" Angela asked.

"That big old Wyoming sky. If you stare all the way around in a circle, in every direction you see sky touching earth. Angel, there's nowhere else in America that you can find a full-circle horizon like that. Nowhere but Wyoming. Other places have trees or mountains or buildings that block the view."

"Uh-huh," Angela muttered, thinking that a few trees or buildings might make the scenery a little bit interesting. For hours they'd been driving along an arrow-straight highway, past a lot of fenced-in nothing.

They'd already stopped to have their picnic lunch. Sitting on the lowered tailgate, dangling their legs, they'd built fat turkey sandwiches. By the time they'd eaten them all the way down to the crusts, their fingers were sticky from mayonnaise and squished tomatoes. When they grabbed a pile of paper napkins to wipe their hands, wind blew the napkins out of the truck. They'd run after the napkins, leaping to catch them, but half of them got stuck on a barbed-wire fence while the rest blew into a pasture.

They'd halted at the fence to inspect the situation. The pasture had lots of sagebrush, some fresh spring grass, a few sleepy cows, and one very mean-looking bull.

"What'll we do?" Angela had asked.

Ant Hil cleared her throat. "Well, I think we should pick up all the napkins we can reach. As for the rest, I'd rather be arrested for littering than get gashed by barbed wire and gored by a bull," she said. "How about you?"

Angela very definitely agreed.

"Then let's beat it out of here before the cops come," Ant Hil said.

Giggling at the thought of police chasing them for littering out there in the middle of nowhere, Angela ran with Ant Hil to the truck. They dumped the napkins in the back, then slammed the tailgate shut. Laughing and yelling, "Hurry! Hurry! Do you hear any sirens?" they'd jumped in and sped away. It was the only time on the whole trip that Ant Hil had driven as fast as the speed limit allowed.

The rest of the time, every other car or truck or tractor trailer on the road passed them because Ant Hil drove so slowly. Sometimes the other drivers turned around to give them angry looks or rude gestures, as though their white Ford truck were taking up more than its share of highway. It was even more embarrassing when other drivers turned around and laughed. Wearing her cowboy hat, clutching the steering wheel, Ant Hil sat perched on the seat with her chin craned high so she could see over the dashboard. From passing cars, she must have looked funny.

"Ant Hil, couldn't we go a little faster?" Angela asked.

"I'm going fifty," Ant Hil answered. "That's fast enough."

"Everyone's passing us!"

"If they want to kill themselves, that's their problem," Ant Hil said. "It's Memorial Day weekend. Drivers are supposed to use more caution on holidays. Anyway, if we go too fast you won't see as much, and I don't want you to miss this magnificent scenery."

Angela gave her a look of unbelief, but Ant Hil really meant it. Holding the steering wheel by only one hand, which was pretty daring for Ant Hil, she reached over to tap a message on Angela's arm in Morse code. Dot dash; dot dash dash; dot; dot dot dot; dash dash dash; dash dash; dot."

Ant Hil had just spelled *awesome* in Morse international code. Angela knew all the dots and dashes for the Morse alphabet; sometimes she and Ant Hil tapped secret messages into each other's hands when they didn't want other people to know what they were thinking. It was the code Ant Hil had used when she'd worked as a telegraph operator for the railroad.

"What's awesome?" Angela asked out loud.

"This Wyoming scenery."

"A few trees would help."

"Yes, but no trees means no pollen. I haven't needed my nasal spray all day. Still, I wish we had time to go to Yellowstone Park over on the other side of Wyoming. Yellowstone's full of trees and beautiful scenery."

"I thought half the park got burned up in those big fires," Angela said.

"That means the other half of the park *didn't* get burned up," Ant Hil told her. "Look on the bright side of things, Angel. Anyway, the newspaper said that some of the foliage is already growing back. Oh, I wish I could show you the bears in Yellowstone. They sit up and beg alongside the road. When your grandmother and I were girls, we fed the bears doughnuts."

"Uh-huh." Angela rested her head on the back of the seat. The highway unwound straight ahead, with not a thing to see on either side except a few pump jacks. Those looked a little bit like dinosaurs, with long necks and oval heads that never stopped turning as they pumped oil from the ground. Pump jacks, some cows—nothing else was out there.

Sunlight glinted on the fine blond hairs on Angela's arms, making them look as if they'd been sprinkled with glitter. She moved her arms in and out of the sun to watch the effect. It was neat, but after a few minutes the sun went behind the clouds.

She propped her arms on the back of the seat and wiggled her fingers. Then made a tight fist, pressed it against her lips, and pretended she was playing a horn. Then she kicked off her shoes.

Sliding around under the seat belt, she managed to slant herself at an angle. Moving only the big toe and the second toe of each foot, she walked her sock toes up the inside of the door and onto the dashboard.

I am bored, she thought. I. Am. Bored. Iambored Iambored Iam *very* bored. She walked her sock toes back down the door.

"Why are you fidgeting?" Ant Hil asked.

She didn't want to hurt Ant Hil's feelings. In a tiny voice she answered, "Bored."

"With this fantastic Wyoming scenery surrounding you? Well, we'll just have to do something to un-bore you, then. I'm going to buy you a surprise."

The truck took a sharp curve that pushed Angela against the armrest. "Where? Here?" she asked. A green and white road sign said CHUGWATER. POPULATION 282. She looked for a town, but all she could see were a few buildings and a dog sleeping in the middle of the road.

"It may not look like much, but this town's famous," Ant Hil said.

"For what?"

"You'll see. Anyway, we need to use the restrooms." Ant Hil pulled the truck to a stop in front of the town's one store. The sign on front said CHUG-WATER GENERAL STORE AND SODA FOUNTAIN.

Inside the small, dimly lighted shop, a woman behind the cash register told Ant Hil the restrooms were in the back. "I won't be more than a minute," Ant Hil whispered to Angela.

Half the store was taken up by a counter with a mirror on the wall and glasses lined up in front of it. Three old cowboys leaned against the counter. Their backs were to Angela, but she could tell they were watching her in the mirror. "Howdy," one said, tipping his big Stetson hat.

"Hi," she answered. All three men had on worn-looking ten-gallon hats, plaid shirts, jeans, and boots. She didn't want to stare, so she looked at a big elk head mounted on the wall. Its antlers spread wide, and its mouth seemed to grin.

"That little blond gal's admirin' you, Wendell," one of the cowboys said.

"Shoot, everyone admires Wendell," another cowboy said. "Every good-lookin' gal that comes in here makes a big fuss over ole Wendell. Yep, all the gals fall for Wendell."

"Yep!" The men grinned and poked one another.

Angela blushed. Couldn't they see she wasn't admiring any of them? Which one was Wendell?

"Don't let those old coots tease you," the woman at the cash register said. "That big old elk on the wall—he's the one named Wendell."

All three cowboys burst into loud laughter and slapped their knees. Just then Ant Hil came back, which gave Angela an excuse to go to the restroom.

When they left the store, the dog was still sleeping in the middle of the road. He hadn't moved. Inside the truck, Ant Hil gave a little bag to Angela and said, "This is what Chugwater is famous for. Wyoming Championship Chugwater Chili Powder!"

"Chili powder?" Angela asked. Some surprise!

"Take it to Texas with you, Angel, because Texans think they know everything there is to know about chili. Show this to the first person who comes up and starts bragging to you about Texas chili."

"Okay." Angela held the plastic bag with the tips of her fingers while they drove carefully around the sleeping dog. The strong odor of chili overpowered the new-car smell. She wrinkled her nose. Chili wasn't one of her favorite foods.

At the highway, signs pointed right for Casper and left for Cheyenne. Ant Hil turned left.

"Aren't we going home now?" Angela asked.

"It's five o'clock and we're only an hour from Cheyenne. I figure we can have dinner in Cheyenne, then still get back to Casper by not too much after ten o'clock tonight," Ant Hil answered.

"Sara's going to wonder why I haven't brought back her sleeping bag."

"It's in the back of the truck."

"In our truck? Sara's sleeping bag?"

"Yes. Yours, too. I brought yours along so we could sit on it while we picnicked, but we stayed on the tailgate, so we didn't need it. We'll drop off Sara's tonight, if her parents are still up when we get back to Casper."

That sounded reasonable. Ant Hil seemed like her old self. She hadn't once done or said anything strange the whole day. Angela was glad now she hadn't mentioned her worries to Sara. They faded like a bad dream as the truck rolled along the ordinary, boring highway, which just kept going, straight and flat.

Wyoming certainly was big.

9

Cheyenne

Stomping and yelling, the cowboys surrounded Ant Hil. "Go, lady, go!" they shouted. "Boy howdy, look at that old gal play! Zap 'im, lady. Ugh! That one was close! I thought that frog was a goner."

Cool, in total control, Ant Hil moved the joystick just enough to maneuver the frog across the highway past speeding cars, through a canal filled with menacing snakes, otters, crocodiles, and treacherous diving turtles.

"She's got twenty-three thousand points already and she's still got three frogs left! Holy sh— ucks!"

"Come on, Grandma! Jump them frogs!" yelled a tall, skinny man in a leather vest.

Not losing a second's concentration, Ant Hil declared, "I'm not anyone's grandma, least of all yours, you big clown! My name is Miss Hilda."

The cowboys hooted with laughter and stomped their boot heels on the wooden floor. "She shot *you* down, Clyde!" they yelled. "Clyde the clown!" They

59

began to clap in time and shout, "Go, Miss Hilda! Go, Miss Hilda! Go, Miss Hilda!"

Angela hung back behind the crowd, half excited and half embarrassed by the fuss Ant Hil was creating. Since she was too short to see Ant Hil or the video screen, she watched, instead, the laughing, keyed-up people in the crowd. Dollar bills passed from hand to hand as Ant Hil's score climbed higher and higher. The cowboys were betting on her! With each level Ant Hil conquered, the crowd became louder and rowdier and the money changed hands faster.

Everyone in the restaurant had by now abandoned their dinners to circle Ant Hil. Even the waiters stopped working. Trays dangled from their hands as they craned their necks to see, over the tall western hats of the cowboys, how large a score the little old lady was piling up.

"Aw . . . ! Dang it!" A groan of disappointment rose from the whole group when Ant Hil's last frog met death from a fast snake.

"That's the most points anyone ever made on this game," one of the waiters said in awe. Everyone applauded then, and they kept it up until they drifted back to their tables and their cold dinners.

"Where's Angel?" Ant Hil cried. "Are you all right, Angel? I couldn't see you. Too many people around."

"I'm fine."

60

"That was fun, wasn't it?" Ant Hil's face looked flushed with excitement, and she sounded breathless. "I guess we'd better order our dinners now, or we'll be awfully late getting back home to Casper."

"Ma'am!" A portly man came up to Ant Hil and said, "I'm Luke Keyser from Spotted Horse, Wyoming, and this here's my grandson Larry."

Next to him stood a boy a few years older than Angela, so blond his eyebrows faded into his face.

"Larry and me," the man said to Ant Hil, "would be real proud if you'd let us buy dinner for you and your granddaughter there."

"This isn't my granddaughter," Ant Hil told him. "She's my grandniece, my Angel."

"Yes, ma'am, she's grand, all right, and that yeller hair and blue eyes surely makes her look like an angel."

"And she acts like one, too!" Ant Hil rattled on, still excited from her success. "Never fusses, never sasses, she's a perfect child. Not like those children you read about today in the newspapers who do such awful things."

Burning with embarrassment, Angela tugged Ant Hil's arm to make her stop. Larry's eyes focused somewhere in the distance. No wonder he didn't want to look at her. She didn't blame him.

Luke Keyser said, "How about it? Would you two join us for dinner?"

Ant Hil tilted her head, silently questioning if it

would be all right with Angela. Angela felt flustered. After all that "perfect" chatter, she didn't know whether she wanted to eat in front of Larry, who was just about the handsomest boy she'd ever seen. What if she spilled something? "Okay," she murmured.

"Fine!" Luke Keyser looked pleased, but Larry didn't look any particular way.

When they were seated in a booth, Ant Hil and Angela opposite Luke Keyser and Larry, a waiter handed them grease-spotted menus. "You know," Luke said, leaning across the table to Ant Hil, "they have Rocky Mountain oysters at this place."

"Rocky Mountain oysters! I haven't had them since I was a young girl."

"What are Rocky Mountain oysters?" Angela asked. She thought she heard Larry give a little snort.

Luke seemed embarrassed. "Uh . . . ," he answered, "when bull calves are turned into steers, the part that's left behind is called Rocky Mountain oysters."

That didn't make sense to Angela, so she thought she'd better not order them, whatever they were. Larry held his menu up over his face. Definite snorts came from behind that menu until Luke gave Larry a poke in the ribs.

"I'll have tacos," Angela decided.

The juke box never stopped playing, mostly sad songs with words like:

Should I come home,
Or should I go crazy?
I'm beggin' you please
To make up your mind. . . .

When they'd almost finished eating, Luke asked, "Miss Hilda, would you care to dance?"

This time it was Ant Hil who got flustered. "Well, I don't want to leave Angel just sitting here. . . ."

"Larry would be pleased to dance with Angel," Luke said. "Wouldn't you, Larry?"

The boy had been mopping up gravy with a chunk of dinner roll. He missed a beat in his chewing, but only one beat. "You bet," he said.

Angela could feel the heat coming into her cheeks. He was being forced to dance with her! Her fists clenched in her lap. Beneath the table, Ant Hil reached to take one of Angela's stiff hands in hers. With her index finger, she tapped onto Angela's palm, in Morse code, "You don't have to. We can leave."

Glancing sideways at her great-aunt, Angela could tell how much she wanted to stay. Ant Hil so seldom got out to have fun; almost never, in fact. Angela went lots of places without Ant Hil—to school, or birthday parties, or to the movies with Sara. Ant Hil never went anywhere much.

"Dot dot; long dash; dot dot dot; dash dash dash; dash dot dash," she tapped back onto Ant Hil's palm. "It's OK." Tapping again, she added, "We'll stay."

Angela had on her stonewashed denim skirt and a white Esprit turtleneck her parents had sent from Albuquerque, so she looked all right on the dance floor. Larry didn't look at her very much, anyway. He was paying attention mostly to his own feet.

Only two other couples were dancing, and one of them was Ant Hil and Luke Keyser, so the floor was nearly empty. Angela felt conspicuous as Larry held her hands and moved completely out of rhythm with the music. Grim and determined, he stumbled along on the wooden floor, and Angela stumbled with him. His straight blond bangs got damp with sweat.

She was surprised that he was such a poor dancer. Didn't they have dances at the school he went to? "Where do you go to school?" she asked. "In Spotted Horse?"

"Naw. I get bused to Gillette."

"What grade are you in?"

"Eighth."

She'd found out how old he was, anyway, or at least she could make a good guess. An eighth grader would be thirteen.

"What grade are you in?" he asked.

She hesitated. "Seventh," she answered, with

just a tiny hitch in her voice. It wasn't exactly a lie, at least not a big one. Only one week of school was left, and then she'd be finished with sixth grade, so that would make her officially a seventh grader. If she told him she was only in sixth, he probably wouldn't want to waste time on her. Anyway, her teachers always said she acted exceptionally mature for her age.

From the jukebox, two female voices lamented:

> *"You've changed, somehow,*
> *You're not my sweet darlin', now,*
> *I'm hurtin', too,*
> *'Cause I'm scared of losin' you."*

Ant Hil and Luke Keyser bounced and swooped and turned in time to the song. Luke dipped his shoulders from side to side while his legs swooshed kind of rubbery, and he pumped Ant Hil's arm up and down. She still wore her cowboy hat; when Luke ducked his head to say things to her, their hat brims bumped. Ant Hil seemed to be having a wonderful time. Her cheeks were all pink, her eyes sparkled, and she never stopped smiling.

Angela was having a less than wonderful time. She and Larry couldn't get their feet to move in the same direction. At dances in Angela's school, the kids never held hands; they just moved separately, facing each other. This was awful! Larry's lips pressed tight in exasperation, as if he wished he were anywhere else except on that dance floor.

"I'm just no dang good at dancing," he burst out. "You probably hate doing this, Angel."

"It's fine," she told him. He was as self-conscious as she was!

"Hey, let's play video games," he suggested. "I'll get some quarters from my grandpa."

"All right!" That would be a lot more fun than stepping all over each other's feet to the song the jukebox was playing now: *Pour me another tequila, Sheila, and put on that fancy red dress.*"

After the first video game was over, Larry said bluntly, "You're not anywhere near as good as that old lady."

"Well, that's rude to say!" she told him.

"Sorry." He blushed even redder than Angela had earlier, but then Larry was a much paler blond. His hair was the kind that turned almost white in the summer. He put another quarter into a karate video game that two people could play, and asked, "Anyway, how'd she get so good at these things?"

"She just has fantastic control," Angela said, forgiving him. "She used to be a telegraph operator for the railroad."

"My grandpa could never do this," Larry told her. "He's good at other things, though, like target shooting."

Larry and Angela were about equal in skill on the karate game. She'd win one time and he'd win the next. It started to be fun. He seemed to like her. She was glad she hadn't told him she was only eleven. After all, she'd be twelve in two months and a week.

"Do you live with your grandpa?" she asked.

"Yeah. Just me and him."

By then she felt comfortable enough to ask, "Your grandfather's pretty old, too. Does he ever do anything, you know, maybe a little . . . strange?"

Larry chuckled. "Yeah. Well, he doesn't do it in front of anybody except me, but sometimes when we're talking. . . . See, he wears false teeth, and sometimes just to be funny he'll push out the bottom ones with his tongue. I mean, I'll be saying something, and those bottom dentures jump out at me. It cracks me up."

Angela had been about to exclaim, "Ooh! Gross!" but she caught herself in time. Larry obviously thought his grandpa's trick was funny.

"That wasn't exactly what I meant," she said. "Does he ever do anything that's . . . like . . . not an ordinary way to act?"

She wasn't paying enough attention to her game. Larry's karate man gave hers a fast sideways kick, and lights flashed all over the board. The game was over—Larry had won.

He leaned on the video machine and said, "Well,

one night I stayed up real late doing my homework. I was so sleepy the next morning that I left for school without it." He propped his chin on his fist and looked straight at Angela. Larry's eyes were blue, with gray rings edging the irises.

"So there I am, talking to the guys on the school bus, when suddenly it swerves and the driver starts cussing. I look out and I see Grandpa standing in the middle of the road, waving my homework papers. He must have driven at warp speed to catch the bus, head it off, and jump out in front of it like that."

Completely caught up in what he was saying, Angela didn't realize at first that Larry had touched her hand. Was still touching it. Deliberately! She became so aware of his fingertips resting on hers that she almost missed the rest of the story.

"All the kids were laughing like crazy. My heck! I wanted to hide under the seat. I didn't need those papers that bad. I'd've only got one grade knocked off for handing them in late. What about Miss Hilda? Does she ever do squirrelly things like that?"

He'd been honest with her, trusted her with his feelings. Could she tell him? Ant Hil said never to discuss family matters with outsiders. But Larry had turned out to be so nice, much nicer than she'd thought he was going to be, and she would probably never see him again. What difference would it make if she told?

No, she couldn't. "Oh, Ant Hil always acts normal," she said.

It was so late when they left the restaurant that Ant Hil decided they'd better spend the night in Cheyenne.

"And sleep in the back of the truck in the sleeping bags?" Angela asked.

"We've had such a wonderful evening, we ought to celebrate. Let's treat ourselves to a motel."

At the Holiday Inn, she surprised Angela by carrying a clothes basket into their room. "I had this week's worth of laundry all ready to put away when we decided to try out the truck, so I brought it along. It's always wise to be prepared for anything, like a change of clothes, in case we'd gotten rained on while we were picnicking. Dig out your pajamas, Angel, and my nightgown."

They hadn't brought toothbrushes, but in the motel bathroom they found a little sign that said the front desk would supply toilet articles on request to guests. So that took care of that.

After she'd changed into her nightgown, Ant Hil said, "I thought people were supposed to be smoking less. Those cowboys must not have got the message—the smoke in that restaurant made my nose stuff up. It was worth it, though. I had such a good time!" She took two allergy pills.

Ant Hil's cheeks were still rosy with pleasure from dancing all evening. She hummed a country-western tune while she brushed her hair. She's pretty, Angela thought. It doesn't matter that she's old—she's really pretty. "Ant Hil, why didn't you ever get married?" she asked.

Seated on one of the beds, her legs tucked under her, Ant Hil answered, "Too independent, I guess. I made good money as a telegrapher during the Depression, when everyone else was broke. And I loved my job. Most men those days expected their wives to stay home after marriage." She plucked at her night-gown, settling it over her knees. "I couldn't see any advantage in marrying an unemployed man just to stay at home and starve with him."

"What about after that?" Angela asked.

"The war came, and all the men went away."

"And after they came back?"

"Get under the covers and I'll tell you."

When Angela slid between the cool white sheets, she realized how sleepy she was. The room had two double beds, and each bed had two pillows. She put both pillows under her head and burrowed backward into them. "Tell me."

Ant Hil turned down her bedspread before she answered, "Your grandmother died then. She was my younger sister, and her husband had left her, so I took her child—your mother—and raised her. We got along just fine. We didn't need a man in the house, or in our lives, either of us."

Speaking into the darkness after she turned off the bedside light, Ant Hil continued, "Not that I didn't have plenty of chances! Lots of men wanted to marry me, but I was content with the way things were. And then . . . "

"Then what?"

"Then, later, came the best part of all. Your parents had to leave Casper to find work, and I got to keep an Angel."

Angela was so drowsy that her words became heavy and slow. "But now I'm leaving you."

"Yes."

As she sank into sleep, she didn't notice Ant Hil's voice grow thick.

"So this is what it's come to. Too darn independent—that's what I've always been. Now I'm going to suffer for it. Left all alone in my old age, with not a soul to love me."

The bed lamp snapped on again, awakening Angela, but only halfway. "What are you doing?" she asked, yawning.

"Getting my nerve pills. Go back to sleep, Angel. I'll see you in the morning."

71

10

Lincoln

Seated on the foot of the Holiday Inn bed, Angela watched television and wondered how long she should let Ant Hil sleep. Since it was Sunday morning, there wasn't anything that interested her on TV, just lots of church programs and some news.

Even though the digital clock on the dresser showed nearly nine, Ant Hil still slept so deeply that she snored. Angela had never heard her snore before. Lightly, then harder and harder, she shook the old woman's shoulder. "Ant Hil, wake up!"

"Hmm?" The eyes opened, but Ant Hil didn't seem really awake. It was as if a curtain had risen on an empty stage.

"Ant Hil, what's the matter?"

"Hmm?" she murmured again. Slowly, she sat up on the edge of the bed.

"I'm hungry, Ant Hil. I called up the front desk, and they said the coffee shop is open. Let's get something to eat. I'm already dressed."

Ant Hil stood up and walked to the door.

"That's the door to the hall!" Angela cried. "The bathroom's over here."

She watched as Ant Hil splashed cold water on her face for a long time. Afterward, to hurry her, Angela picked clothes out of the clothes basket—underwear, slacks, a blouse—and helped her put them on. When she got her out of the room and into the hallway, Ant Hil couldn't tell which direction to take. Angela had to lead her to the coffee shop.

"Orange juice, eggs, and sausage," Angela told the waitress. "Is that what you'd like too, Ant Hil?"

When Ant Hil didn't answer, Angela said to the waitress, "That's what she always has when we go out for breakfast. And she has coffee, too."

"I'll bring the coffee to her right away," the woman said.

After the waitress left, Angela said, "You certainly are tired this morning, Ant Hil. That dancing must have worn you out last night. When we get home, you can take a nice, long nap."

The waitress brought two glasses of juice and a cup of coffee. Stiffly, Ant Hil reached for the juice glass. She knocked it over.

"Whoops! Don't worry about it, honey," the waitress told her. "No problem, as long as it doesn't get on you." The woman ran for a wipe-up cloth as the pool of orange juice spread across the tabletop. Angela tried to dam it with a wad of paper napkins, but Ant Hil just sat there, dazed. Sleepy, that's all—she's just sleepy, Angela told herself.

"I'll bring you another glass of juice," the waitress said after she'd mopped the tabletop. She went away carrying the dripping rag.

Frowning, Ant Hil stared at her coffee cup and picked up a spoon. With a clang, the spoon fell to the floor. Angela scrambled to pick it up.

"What's wrong with you, Ant Hil?" she whispered.

Ant Hil tried to pick up a fork, but she dropped that, too. Then, bending forward from the waist, she lowered her head to the cup on the table and put her lips to the rim.

"Ant Hil!"

The coffee shop, which had buzzed with the low chatter of breakfasters, became suddenly silent. Everyone stared at the old woman who had her face in the coffee.

"Ant Hil, please don't do that!" Angela whispered again, but Ant Hil ignored her.

"Please!" Miserable, Angela huddled in the corner of the booth. The Alzheimer's had come back! Ant Hil raised her dripping face to stare around in confusion.

"Is she all right?" the waitress asked when she brought their food. "Can I get her anything?"

Angela shook her head and reached across the table to dry Ant Hil's chin with a napkin.

"Want more coffee, honey?" The waitress filled Ant Hil's cup without waiting for a reply, then winked at Angela.

This time Ant Hil lifted the cup a little way from the saucer, but it clattered so much she put it back down.

"What's wrong?" Angela whispered again while she watched Ant Hil's hands fumble with the saucer. Last night those lightning fingers had built up the highest score ever recorded on a difficult video game. Today they couldn't even hold a coffee cup.

Slowly, after a time, the dazed look began to lift from Ant Hil's eyes. Although she picked up the sausages with her fingers, she managed to eat the scrambled eggs with a fork. When she'd finished them she asked, "Why aren't you eating, Angel? Your breakfast is getting cold."

She sounded almost normal, but Angela was too upset to believe the incident might be over. "I'm not hungry."

The waitress, who was keeping an eye on them, returned to pour more coffee for Ant Hil. "Do you want a glass of milk or something, honey?" she asked, meaning Angela—she seemed to call everyone honey.

"She's my grandniece, my Angel, and I love her," Ant Hil said.

"I'm sure you do." The woman patted Ant Hil's hand. "I had a real sweet old aunt myself once, when I was a little girl. I still miss her sorely."

"Loneliness is a dreadful thing," Ant Hil declared. Sitting up straighter, she added, "But we have to bear what life sends us." This time she lifted the coffee cup with no trouble.

Softly, the waitress said to Angela, "Let me bring you some warm toast, honey. You really ought to eat something." Then she whispered, as though Ant Hil had gone deaf as well as weird, "The old lady seems all right now. She must have had a few little nips too many before breakfast."

"No!" Angela said, hating it that the waitress felt sorry for her, hating that the woman thought Ant Hil was drunk. "She was just tired," she said.

By the time they started out in the truck, Ant Hil seemed perfectly normal, but when they reached the intersection where the sign pointed the way to Casper, she turned in the opposite direction.

"Aren't we going home?" Angela cried. Every unexpected action now filled her with fear.

"There's something really special I want to show you, Angel, to share with you, and it's not far from here. I'd hate you to miss seeing it before you leave Wyoming for good."

"What is it?" Angela asked, tense, sitting as far forward as the seat belt would allow.

Ant Hil didn't tell her. She only said, "You've never gotten to see the best Wyoming sights because you're only here from September to May, when the weather is too uncertain for traveling. Wyoming has four seasons—June, July, August, and winter."

Was that confused talk, or just a joke? Angela listened carefully to everything Ant Hil said, trying to decide what was normal and what sounded suspicious.

She drove at her usual speed of fifty miles per hour, but now they were on a four-lane interstate where the speed limit was sixty-five. In the left lane, huge tractor trailers passed them. Ant Hil slowed down even more as she searched for whatever it was she wanted to show Angela. Almost every minute a horn blared at them, dropping in pitch as the truck or car whizzed by.

At the highest point on Interstate 80, where the elevation was 8,640 feet, she shouted, "There it is!" Even before they left the turnoff to reach the visitors' parking lot, Angela could see it: a tall pillar, with a bronze bust at the top.

"Abraham Lincoln," Ant Hil announced. "My favorite president! Let's get out and say hello to him."

Angela glanced at her sharply, but it had only been a playful remark. Ant Hil walked with brisk, sure steps to the front of the monument. For a few silent moments they stood gazing up at the craggy bronze face of Lincoln, silhouetted against a brilliant blue sky. Far in the distance, mountain peaks rose in waves of different colors. Wind blew the fresh scent of pines around them, lifting their hair. Two perfectly normal tourists admiring a monument, but Angela chewed one of her knuckles raw.

"I hope you'll remember this always," Ant Hil told her.

"I will. I'll never forget this day." But not because of the scenery or Lincoln.

When they drove back to the highway, Angela peered through the windshield. "Isn't this the direction we were heading in before we went to see the statue?" she asked. "Why didn't you turn around so we can go home?"

"At this point," Ant Hil said, "it's about even steven, the same distance if we go back the way we came or if we drive west to Rawlins, turn north, and loop back to Casper on Route 220. If we take that route we'll get to see some different scenery."

"I've seen enough scenery!" Angela cried. "I want to go home." Before Ant Hil freaked out again. Even if it were true about Casper being the same distance forward or backward, she'd feel safer going home the way they'd come.

"Don't be such a grouch! Look at all this, Angel! Isn't it beautiful? Sing with me! 'When it's springtime in the Rockies, I'll be coming back to you. . . . ' Come on, sing! You have such a lovely voice. Please! For me!"

At school, Angela always got picked for solos in

the glee club programs, but now her voice shook. *"When it's springtime in the Rockies,"* she sang,

> *"With your bonnie eyes of blue,*
> *Once again I'll say I love you,*
> *While the birds sing all the day,*
> *When it's springtime in the Rockies,*
> *In the Rockies, far away."*

At the last line, Angela burst into tears. Quickly, Ant Hil swerved the truck to the shoulder of the road and stopped. "Dear child, what's the matter?" she asked.

"Next year when it's springtime in the Rockies I *won't* be coming back to you."

Ant Hil patted her head as if she were a small child. "There there, we'll reach Laramie soon—it's just up ahead. We'll stop there and I'll buy you something nice."

"I don't want you to buy me anything! I just want you to come live in El Paso with us."

"Angel, I've told you that wouldn't work," Ant Hil said, looking as if she wanted to cry, too. She reached on the floor for her purse and handed it to Angela. "Here. Take out some Kleenex and dry your eyes."

As Angela groped for the tissues, Ant Hil told her, "If you see my pill bottle in there, get it out for me, will you?"

"Your allergy pills?"

"No. Nerve pills. There it is. Hand me that little bottle."

When Angela put it into Ant Hil's hand, she noticed the label. "That isn't your name on the bottle," she said.

"No, it isn't. Our neighbor, Mrs. Garnet, gave these to me. She knew I was a bit upset about you leaving, and she said these pills helped her husband when he got depressed over losing his job. I'll only take one this time."

She swallowed the pill without water and smiled at Angela. "Feeling better?" she asked.

When Angela nodded, Ant Hil said, "Then let's go." She started the truck and drove back onto the highway.

It began to rain before they'd gone too far past the Lincoln monument. Ant Hil said, "There's one good thing about Wyoming weather. If you don't like it, just wait a few minutes and it will change."

"I don't mind the rain," Angela said. The spring shower lasted less than half an hour, and after that a mist rose above the highway. Angela felt as though she were in a cocoon with Ant Hil, as though there were no passing of time, as if they might go on forever that way, hurling down a corridor in the cab of the truck, with big tractor trailers blocking them on the left and road markers keeping them from drifting off to the right.

She jerked alert. They were drifting, all right. To the left! The side of a tractor trailer got closer and closer. "Ant Hil!" Angela screamed, but they kept bearing left, so close to the tractor trailer that Angela could see scratches in its paint. Its horn blared loudly as the driver tried to swerve his big load away from them.

Angela grabbed the steering wheel and jerked it to the right, making their Ford lurch toward the shoulder of the road. Then it was off the road, careening wildly on the soft dirt as it headed into a stand of tall pines.

Clutching the steering wheel with her left hand, Angela unlatched her seat belt with her right and jumped with both feet onto the brake pedal. The Ford swayed from side to side, throwing her around the truck cab, but she hung onto the steering wheel and kept stomping on the brakes. Finally the truck rolled to a stop with its front bumper only inches from a tree trunk, leaving scooped-out tire grooves in the soft dirt behind.

Panting hard, Angela let herself drop back onto the seat. With her fingers she felt her arms and her legs, but nothing seemed hurt.

"I'm so tired," Ant Hil said. "I just can't keep my eyes open." She curled on the seat like a baby, and laid her head in Angela's lap.

11
Waiting

What'll I do? What'll I do? Angela didn't know who she was asking. There was no one to talk to.

While Ant Hil napped peacefully on the truck seat, Angela sat beneath the branches of the pine that had nearly killed them. I can't drive home, she told herself. I can't drive, period. I don't know how I even stopped the truck. Can Ant Hil drive? When she wakes up she might be crazy again. I won't be able to stand it if she is because I'm already scared to death. Death. Both of us nearly died. How will we get home?

Angela hurt, but not from bumping around inside the careening truck. Her ache came from desperately wanting to hear her parents' voices. They telephoned every Sunday, and this was Sunday. In the empty house in Casper, the telephone would be ringing and ringing, with no one there to answer it.

What should I do? she asked herself again. Run out on the highway and try to flag a police car? Then what? Tell the police what happened? Ant Hil might get locked up in the same awful nursing home as Sara's grandmother, where everything smelled sour and the old people looked dirty.

There was nothing she could do but wait. Wait for Ant Hil to wake up. Wait to see how she was. Wait for the next thing to happen. Angela herself couldn't make anything happen—she was too young, too helpless. A kid. Kids were controlled by adults. But what were they supposed to do if the adults went out of control?

Only wait. As Ant Hil had said, "If you wait long enough, the Wyoming weather will change to something you like better." The mist blew away, and the blue sky became hung with billowy clouds like fresh laundry on a clothesline.

"Angel?"

Ant Hil's legs appeared through the truck door.

"My goodness, was I ever sleepy!"

Instantly Angela knew that Ant Hil was all right. Her eyes looked sane, as though she'd taken up residence inside her head once more. She sounded bright and reasonable.

"Do you know what happened?" Angela demanded, her own voice climbing in leftover panic. "First we nearly crashed into a truck, and then we nearly crashed into these trees!"

"What are you talking about, Angel? I just got sleepy, so I pulled over to take a little rest. That's what drivers are supposed to do when they get sleepy. I feel much better now, although I have quite a headache, and you're not helping it any when you shout at me that way."

"You mean you don't remember!" Angela's voice grew shriller.

"Remember what? Maybe you were sleeping, too, and you had a bad dream."

It was a bad dream, all right. A nightmare that was still going on. Ant Hil stretched her arms high over her head, then brought them down and looked at her wristwatch. "What time is it? Gracious! It's late. I think we'd better spend the night at a trailer court in Rawlins."

"No!" Angela yelled. "I want to go home!"

"Dear child, it's only a few hours' drive from Rawlins to Casper. We'll wake up early tomorrow morning and be on the road before sunup. This is a holiday weekend, Angel! Lighten up and have a little fun!"

"Fun!" she screamed. "After you nearly killed us? You were awful in the coffee shop this morning, too! You scared me! You kept dropping things, and you stuck your face in the coffee!"

"Oh, Angel, really! I was just sleepy this morning, too. You said it yourself—I tired myself out with all that dancing. Why are you making such a fuss? It's not like you to act this way."

She seemed so sure of herself that Angela began

to doubt her own certainty. "No, everything you're saying is wrong," she shouted. "I'm right, you're wrong. You didn't pull over, I did it! I could see a scratch on the truck—"

"On our truck? There's a scratch?"

"No, the big truck. The one passing us. Maybe it was a moving van—I don't remember—it was just big. Huge! If we'd hit it—if it had hit us—we'd be splattered! Dead meat!"

Ant Hil frowned, seeming annoyed. Rarely, if ever, could Angela remember Ant Hil looking at her that way. "Get control of yourself, Angel," she said. "You're all worked up. I don't appreciate you criticizing my driving. I've driven for sixty years and I've never even come close to having an accident. Now do as I say and get back into the truck. We'll forget this little outburst so we can enjoy the rest of the trip."

After a minute, Angela did it. Got back into the truck. She had no choice. Kids did what grown-ups told them to. That was how it was to be a kid.

12

Independence

At the recreation vehicle park in Rawlins, where they spent Sunday night in sleeping bags in the back of the truck, Ant Hil acted just fine.

Early Monday morning she told Angela, "I want us to make just one stop on the way back to Casper. There's a very special place I'd like you to see, and it's right along the highway, so it won't take long. Since today is Memorial Day, it's appropriate that you see a bit of Wyoming history."

"No!" Angela said. "I want to go home."

"Angel, this is *on the way* home."

"I don't care. I don't want to stop anywhere." Tears filled her eyes and spilled down her cheeks.

Ant Hil had started the truck. When she noticed the tears, she said, "Honestly, Angel, you're getting as bad as Sara."

"Don't call my best friend bad!" Angela cried.

"You know I didn't mean *bad* bad. I meant she's emotional, and you're beginning to get that way too.

I don't understand why you've suddenly begun behaving like this." She paused. "Have you noticed any body changes lately? Maybe you're getting ready to start your—"

"I'm fine! You're the one who's been acting impossible."

Ant Hil would never ordinarily take her eyes off the road for more than a second, but now she gave Angela a long look. "You'd better rethink that, Angel," she said. "I seem to be the only person in this truck who's in control of herself."

That was true. Ant Hil was in better shape than Angela, who'd gone from pinching her knuckles to chewing them. When they got too sore, she sucked on them. At least she wasn't bored anymore. Too scared to be bored, she crouched in the corner of the seat.

Clear eyed and calm, Ant Hil sat straight with her chin held high to see through the windshield. The Alzheimer's seemed to come and go without predictability. Angela counted—fourteen hours since the last outbreak. When would it begin again? An hour from now? A minute? She kept a wary eye on the two-lane highway to make sure the Ford didn't drift to the right or the left.

To show she held no ill feelings, Ant Hil reached across to tap Angela's arm. Dash dash dash dot dot; dash dash dash dot dot. It spelled 88, the telegraphers' signal for "love and kisses."

Well, okay, Angela thought. "One more stop, and you have to promise to keep it short."

Even though it was a holiday, there were no other cars on the road. Nothing much to see on the sides of the road, either. Earlier they'd passed a big oil well, but now they drove along mile after mile of barbed wire that fenced in acres of yellow dirt and sagebrush. Who could have strung all that wire, Angela wondered. Who could have cut the trees to make all those fence posts? And why would anyone want to fence off so much nothing? She was tired because she hadn't been able to sleep much the night before, and the hum of the tires and the pleasant new-car smell lulled her. It wasn't long until she fell asleep.

The pull of the truck swerving off the highway wakened her, but before she had a chance to panic Ant Hil announced, "Here we are." The truck had come to a stop in a paved lot.

Since someone had gone to all the trouble of paving a parking lot out there in the middle of nowhere, there must be something for people to visit, but all Angela could see was an enormous rock mound shaped like a bread loaf. "What is it?" she asked, rubbing her eyes. The nap had made her feel a little better.

"Independence Rock. The most important resting place on the old Oregon Trail. Thousands upon thousands of pioneers stopped here on their way to California, and most of them carved their names on the rock in a living memorial. Wait till you see it, Angel! It makes you feel as if all those pioneers passed through only yesterday."

She had to trot to keep up with Ant Hil. At a small wooden footbridge, a sign proclaimed that ruts from pioneer wagons could still be seen beneath the bridge, but if they were there, Angela couldn't make them out. When they reached the foot of the rock, which towered high above them, Ant Hil clapped her hands and cried, "Look at the names, Angel!"

"I see some," Angela answered. "It says, 'Tim and Sharon, 1983.' "

"What! Where?" Ant Hil's delight drained away. "Heavens! Vandals have defaced Independence Rock. I can't believe it! Good gracious! Why don't the police do something about it?"

Police! Way out there, Angela would have been surprised to see any sign of life at all, even a sheep, let alone a policeman. But Ant Hil looked so horrified that Angela felt sorry for her. To cheer her, she said, "There's a much older date over to the left. See? Nineteen fifty-two."

"Nineteen fifty-two!" Ant Hil spat out the numbers as though they were gnats. "When I came

89

here as a girl, I could find dates from *eighteen* fifty-two!"

Angela began to search carefully for older dates, scrambling up the sloping sides of the sandstone to see better. "Here's a really old one," she called out. "Nineteen thirty-seven."

"Humpf!"

Climbing higher, she made a real find. "Look, Ant Hil! This one's *ancient.* It says, 'H. Fisk, 1911.' That's even before you were born."

"Not by much!" Ant Hil shot back. Age lines radiated like thin spokes from her pursed lips. "You'd better come down from there now, Angel, before you fall and hurt yourself. It's no use looking. It's just a waste of time."

Angela hesitated. It had become interesting to read the scratchings on the rock. "Class of 1992." "Todd loves Jessica." "Jesus Saves." But she was the one who'd wanted to keep the stop short, she remembered. She ran down the rough, curved surface to Ant Hil, who said dejectedly, "I just can't understand what happened to all the pioneer names. The last time I visited here, you could see hundreds of them, and dates from as far back as the eighteen-sixties."

"When was that, Ant Hil?" Angela asked. "When did you last visit here?"

"Before the war."

"Which war?"

"The real war. The important war. World War Two."

They'd reached the parking lot, where Angela stopped between two historical markers. "Well, no wonder then. That was fifty years ago. Look what it says here on this marker. 'Almost all of the pioneer names are now covered with lichen, Mother Nature's own eraser, which is decomposing the rock.' "

Ant Hil stood with her hands on her hips. "It's bad enough that the rock is decomposing, but why do people insist on vandalizing our national treasures? I brought you here to show you some Wyoming history, not a bunch of modern graffiti!"

Angela was tempted to point out that today's graffiti might be tomorrow's history, but she decided she'd better not. Ant Hil looked too discouraged. She was moving like an old woman. Even though Angela had been angry and exasperated with her only an hour before, now she ran around to help her into the truck.

"There's one place I'm sure hasn't changed," Ant Hil muttered as she turned the key in the ignition. "One thing you can count on *never* to change." As soon as Angela ran back and climbed inside the truck, Ant Hil yanked the gearshift.

The lurch of the truck knocked an almost empty soda can off the dashboard, spilling a little cola over the floor mat on Angela's side. Bending down to mop up the spill with Kleenex, she didn't notice Ant Hil turn west at the highway.

Casper lay to the east.

Not until it was too late to turn back did Angela learn they were on their way to Yellowstone Park.

By then she was too tired to fight anymore, too weary from all the worrying to make any further fuss. Besides, Ant Hil had been fine for nineteen hours and counting. Maybe all the trouble was behind them.

Or maybe not. Angela could only hope. She had to give up the fear and give in to what was happening, because there was nothing she could do about it anyway. Ant Hil was so sweet all the time that you hardly realized she always did exactly what she pleased.

Come to think of it, that's what Angela's parents did, too. They were wonderful to her, but they made all their decisions without consulting her. Jerked around like a puppet—that seemed to be Angela's place in the space of things. The grown-ups petted her, pampered her, and spoiled her enough to disguise the fact that they completely controlled her.

If only this hadn't been Memorial Day weekend! On any ordinary Monday she'd have been sitting at her desk in Casper, in the classroom with her friends, which was where she wanted to be. "Promise me we won't stay more than just overnight in Yellowstone," she begged. "Promise me we'll go home tomorrow, first thing in the morning."

"I just want you to see Old Faithful," Ant Hil answered. "In this whole changing world, it's the one thing that always stays the same. That's why it's called Old Faithful."

Angela sighed and rolled her head back against the seat. One more stop; one more overnight. If only Ant Hil stayed sane, they'd be back in Casper before this time tomorrow. Early enough that she could get to school for at least part of the day. It was her last week.

13

Yellowstone

" 'The terrible fires of the summer of 1988,' " Angela read out loud, " 'burned more than a million acres of Yellowstone National Park. Impacted were many prime feeding areas for large animals, especially the bears.' "

A ranger had given them the newspaper, called *Yellowstone Today,* when they paid their entry fee at the park gate. Angela folded it to the next column and continued, " 'Much of the vegetation has by now grown back, but the bear . . . ' What's that word—hab . . . itat?"

"Habitat. I think that means where they usually live."

" ' . . . will not reach a stable condition again for several more seasons. Grizzly bears are still ranging far and wide to establish new territories. This creates a higher than usual possibility for bear-human conflicts.' "

For the first few miles after they'd come into the

94

park through South Entrance, they'd seen no sign of fire damage. "What did I tell you?" Ant Hil had asked, pleased. "It's just the way I remember it."

The living pines wore most of their greenery on their tops, with their lower trunks naturally barren. Many had fallen over—not burned, just dead of natural causes. Some of the silver-colored trunks never hit the ground when they died. Neighboring trees caught them and held them at odd angles.

Ant Hil said, "These trees are called lodgepole pines because that's what the Indians used them for—to prop up their tepees. Thank heavens I don't seem to be allergic to their pollen."

Abruptly the green forest ended, and they drove into an area that had been torched by the inferno. For the next several miles they passed tree skeletons standing straight up with all their branches burned off. Charred and bare, they looked like blackened toothpicks on parade. Ant Hil grew silent. Her lips pressed into a somber line.

"So I guess what I just read," Angela said to break the silence, "means that a lot of bears are wandering around looking for new places to eat because their old places got burned."

"I wish they'd wander closer to the road so we could see some," Ant Hil said. "They used to line the roads here. People would get out of their cars and feed them."

"It says you're not supposed to feed the bears,"

Angela told her. She shuffled through a pile of folders the rangers had given them in addition to the newspaper. "It says here, 'Bears are dangerous. They may attack for no apparent reason. Bears can seriously injure or kill people. Please take every precaution.' "

"Oh, posh!" said Ant Hil. "When we were girls, your grandmother and I came here each summer with our father. Every evening whole crowds of people would gather around to watch grizzlies eat at the garbage dumps. We used to feed them by hand."

"Not anymore," Angela said. "You're not allowed to feed them."

"Then I can understand why the poor things no longer come alongside the road. No one's giving them anything to eat."

After a number of miles they drove out of the scorched earth into green forest once again. Ant Hil visibly perked up, but Angela was growing tired from the long drive. On Yellowstone's twisting, two-lane highway, their truck barely crept along. It wasn't Ant Hil's fault; for a change she didn't drive any more slowly than anyone else. The narrow, no-passing road was full of cars, vans, campers, huge fifth-wheel trailers, darting bicycles, and noisy motorcycles. Angela peered out at the bumper-to-bumper vehicles and wondered why so many people wanted to be in Yellowstone Park on Memorial Day.

Whenever the park visitors spotted wild animals

in a meadow, they would stop their cars, jump out, and take pictures, which caused all the other vehicles to pile up in traffic jams. Ant Hil always slowed down to see what kind of animal was causing the jam-up. "Drat!" she'd say. "It's only elk." Buffalo disappointed her just as much. "It's bears I want you to see, Angel. Keep looking for them."

Angela didn't see any bears, but she finally spotted the signpost they were searching for. "There's the turnoff to Old Faithful," she announced. "At last!"

Ant Hil turned at the intersection and pulled into a huge parking lot, bigger than any Angela had ever seen, even at a Dallas shopping mall. "It's so long since I've been here that I've forgotten where Old Faithful actually is," Ant Hil told her as they got out of the truck.

"There's a visitors' center," Angela answered. "We can find out inside."

The visitors' center was filled with exhibits about geysers and thermal pools and mud pots and wildlife. A new-looking display showed the order in which plants grow back after a devastating fire. Above an information counter hung a sign that said "OLD FAITHFUL MAY ERUPT AT 4:21."

"Excuse me," Ant Hil said to the ranger behind the counter, "what does that mean—*may* erupt at 4:21? Don't you know exactly when it's going to erupt?"

"No, ma'am," the ranger answered. "It could go off ten minutes early or ten minutes late or any time in between."

"That's ridiculous," Ant Hil said. "Old Faithful has always been punctual."

"Afraid not, ma'am," he said. "The time between eruptions can last anywhere from 46 to 85 minutes, or even longer. They've kept records for eighty years, and it's always been like that."

"You're wrong," she said. "When I came here as a girl, Old Faithful was always on time. Are you a regular park ranger?"

"I'm a summer temporary," he answered.

"Well, no wonder, then. After you get more experience, you'll learn these things." She smiled at him kindly.

The ranger opened his mouth as if he wanted to answer, but then he changed his mind. As they left the visitors' center Ant Hil held Angela's arm and whispered, "The park shouldn't hire people who don't know anything about Old Faithful. Why does that young man think it's called Old Faithful, for heaven's sake!"

Several hundred people sat outside on circular benches, waiting for the next eruption. Ant Hil dug her fingers into Angela's arm and steered her past the rows of benches to the very front seats. "I want you to have a perfect view of this spectacular sight," she explained when Angela tried to hold back, embarrassed about pushing in front of people who were already there.

The late-afternoon sun drifted in and out from high white clouds. Angela held a hand above her eyes, but Ant Hil's face was shaded by the brim of her western hat. Small wisps of steam drifted up from the mouth of the geyser several hundred yards in the distance. "Is that it?" Angela asked.

"That little puff! Goodness, no. When Old Faithful goes off, it sprays a big, high spout right up into the sky."

Angela didn't have a watch, but Ant Hil looked at hers often. "It's now 4:23," she said. "What was it that sign said in the visitors' center?"

"That it might be ten minutes late if it wasn't ten minutes early," Angela answered.

"No, not what the ranger said. I mean the actual time printed on the sign."

"Four twenty-one."

Ant Hil shook her watch. "I wonder if I forgot to wind it this morning. It seems to be running fast."

"If you forgot to wind it, it should be slow," Angela told her.

The minutes crept past. Ant Hil still looked at her watch, but now she'd stopped saying anything. Her lips tightened as if to hold back the complaints she really wanted to make, which wouldn't have been patriotic, since Old Faithful was an American institution.

The people sitting around them were beginning to make jokes, suggesting that maybe there was a little man down there who was supposed to turn on the steam, but he'd gone off on his dinner break. Or that maybe the show had been canceled because of poor ticket sales. Ant Hil was not amused. At 4:31 she squinted at the jokers and said, "Everyone tries so hard to be a comedian!"

Angela scrunched her shoulders and ducked her head, but no one seemed to take offense—they just laughed. Maybe they thought anyone that old had a right to say whatever she pleased. And Ant Hil wasn't finished. At 4:35 she declared, "This is really outrageous! It's a national disgrace!"

"You tell 'em, lady!" someone yelled. "If this wasn't free, I'd ask for my money back."

Everyone laughed again. Everyone except Ant Hil was taking the delay with good humor. A few people nudged one another, amused at the indignant old woman in the cowboy hat. Fists on hips, cheeks pink with annoyance, she didn't try to hide her disapproval of the way nature was running things in Yellowstone National Park.

At 4:37 Angela said, "I think it's starting. It is, Ant Hil! It's starting." People began to cheer.

With a loud hissing and noisy splashes, a white column of steam and water thrust higher and higher into the blue sky. "Ant Hil, it's wonderful. It was worth waiting for," Angela exclaimed.

"I suppose so." Ant Hil tried to frown, but her resentment slipped away as the superheated water climbed up, up . . . to a hundred forty feet, bigger and far more spectacular than any man-made fountain. "It is beautiful, isn't it? What did I tell you, Angel? Keep looking—it isn't over yet."

The display continued, peaked, then began to grow smaller. Underground, the pressure of the steam decreased; aboveground, the geyser became lower and leaner. After the last bit of spray fell back to the earth, Ant Hil checked her watch. "Four minutes—is that all?" she asked. "When I was a girl, it lasted much longer than that. Still," she declared happily, "it was as beautiful as I ever remembered."

"Everything is filled up—all three hundred rooms here at Old Faithful Inn and all the cabins outside," said the young woman behind the desk. "It's a holiday, you know."

"We'll just have to camp, then," Ant Hil told Angela. She sounded tired. "We can sleep in the back of our truck."

"There's no campground here at Old Faithful, and you may have trouble finding space anywhere else. Several campgrounds have been closed because of grizzly bear sightings. Let me make a few phone calls." The clerk's manner softened as she glanced at Ant Hil. "Why don't you sit in the lobby in that big easy chair? As soon as I find out anything, I'll come and tell you."

Ant Hil sank gratefully into the overstuffed Naugahyde, and Angela sat cross-legged on the floor beside her.

"Tired?" Ant Hil asked.

"Sure. Aren't you?" Angela stroked Ant Hil's thin, veined hand and said, "That was a long, long drive today."

"Oh no, I'm not tired at all. I'm fine." She smiled brightly.

It wasn't long before the reservations clerk came to tell them, "There are a still a couple of spaces left at Norris Campground, but you'll have to hurry because they're first-come, first-served."

"What about food? Is there a restaurant there?"

"No, ma'am. If I were you, I'd grab a hamburger here at the concession, and then drive as fast as possible to Norris."

"All right. Thank you, miss." She smiled again, a smile that seemed harder to call up each time she used it. Then she said, "Would you help me up, please, Angel? I think this chair is trying to swallow me."

Angela felt a pinch of fear, but Ant Hil was just being witty.

14

Norris

They got the last camping spot at Norris, the end space on Loop C. The fires that scorched Yellowstone in the summer of 1988 had skipped around, torching the forests in patches. This mosaic pattern of burning left Norris campground green and unseared, an oasis among the surrounding charred acres. Overhead, lodgepole pines swayed in the wind to brush each other's green branches like friends. The breeze swept gently past Angela's cheeks and ruffled Ant Hil's hair beneath her hat brim.

Ant Hil dug into her purse and came up with a twenty-dollar bill. "Angel, would you take this to the ranger cabin and pay our campground fee?" she asked. "Did you see the cabin when we drove in? It's just past the little bridge."

"Sure," Angela said. A walk would feel good after all that sitting in the truck.

Before she knocked at the cabin door, she stopped to read a big yellow poster tacked to the outside wall. "Bears need your CONCERN, not your food," it said. "Store food properly. Avoid surprise encounters. Stay out of areas of heavy grizzly activity."

A dark-haired young ranger answered her knock. He wasn't tall, but he had broad, muscular shoulders and long arms.

"I want to pay the campground fee," Angela said, holding up the twenty.

"Sorry, I don't have enough change—the fee's only seven dollars," he explained. Through the screen door, Angela could see a name tag, "Phil," pinned to his gray uniform shirt. A brown patch on the sleeve said "National Park Service." From a strap around his neck hung a police whistle; the strap looked like something his girlfriend might have woven for him out of gray plastic laces.

"Tell you what, my partner should be back here in a little while," he said. "She'll come to collect your fee. What space are you in?"

"The end on Loop C."

"Okay. Look for a ranger named Becky."

"Good evening, folks," Becky began, speaking what sounded like a recorded message. "Welcome to Norris Campground. You need to know that this is grizzly bear country. We ask you to make sure that all your food and food storage items are secured inside your vehicle. Do not leave them outside. This includes items such as knives, forks, spoons, plates, dog food, cat food—"

"Cat food!" Ant Hil exclaimed. "We don't have a cat."

". . . any food scraps," Becky went on, "or deodorant, toothpaste—"

"Toothpaste!"

"Yes, ma'am. Whatever smells good to a bear—and that means just about everything—has to be stowed safely away. I see you have a Styrofoam food cooler in the back of your truck."

Angela said, "It's empty. We threw everything away after lunch today. It was getting stale."

"Still," Becky told them, "that Styrofoam has food odors in it, so you need to store it inside your vehicle tonight. Food odors attract bears."

"Are there really any bears left around here?" Ant Hil asked, as though she doubted it. "We haven't seen a single one since we got to Yellowstone, and I really wanted Angel to see some and maybe get a chance to feed one like I used to do."

Becky looked incredulous. "Feed one! You want the kid to feed a bear?" She no longer sounded like a public service announcement. Almost sputtering, she said, "In the first place, that's illegal. In the second place, it's about the most dangerous thing she could do!"

Ant Hil tossed her head and said, "I find that

hard to believe. When I was a girl, we always fed the bears in the park and they never hurt anyone."

"I'm not sure when that might have been," Becky said, "but before the bear policy changed in 1970, an average of forty-eight people a year got injured here in Yellowstone by bears looking for handouts. Now that people aren't allowed to feed them, the number of injuries has gone way down."

"And Yellowstone is a lot less fun to visit." Ant Hil sniffed. "It used to be so cute to see the bears begging."

Becky took off her ranger hat. She rubbed her forehead as if she were trying to figure out how to deal with this visitor from another era. "It was never much fun for the bears," she said. "It was degrading to them, and unhealthy. You seem to be someone who likes bears, right? Well, the sad thing is that when bears would hurt people, we usually ended up having to kill the bears."

Ant Hil had taken the sleeping bags out of the back of the truck. She opened them so they could air, then busied herself shaking the pillows to show she wasn't taking the ranger too seriously.

Becky turned to Angela. "I'm not trying to scare you folks," she said, "but we've had bear sightings near some of the other campgrounds this week. It's good that you have a hard-sided camper. We won't let anyone sleep in tents now because bears can slash

106

right through canvas. And we're being extra strict about food storage."

Angela remembered she'd left part of a Snickers bar in the truck. Wide-eyed, she asked, "What should you do if a bear comes after your food? Or after *you?*"

Becky hitched herself up to sit beside Angela on the tailgate of the truck, and set her ranger hat between them. Tall and thin, she wore her straight black hair in a ponytail fastened by elastics. Her uniform was identical to the one Phil wore: gray shirt and green slacks, with no difference in style between men's and women's. She took off her sunglasses before she answered, "There's nothing you can do that's guaranteed safe. I mean, I could tell you some rules, but bears don't go by any rules."

"Tell me anyway."

"Well . . . okay. First, you absolutely don't run. If you do, a bear will chase you for sure, and no human can win a race against a bear."

"What else?" Angela asked. It was scary hearing all these things, but it was kind of nice to talk to someone under seventy for a change.

"You could throw something down to distract the bear. A backpack or a camera—the bear might stop to investigate it. Or try climbing a tree if there's a tall one nearby. If all else fails, you lie down curled up in a cannonball position with your hands on the back of your neck." Becky demonstrated, lacing her fingers behind her neck. "See? You try it. When you're lying facedown with your hands like this, it makes it harder for a bear to bite through your neck."

"Oh, for heaven's sake!" Ant Hil exploded. "What an awful thing to say to a child!"

Becky reddened and shifted on the tailgate. "I wasn't trying to frighten her," she apologized. "Everything I just said is in the brochures you got when you entered the park." As if to make amends, she leaned closer to Angela and said, "Bears don't always hurt you when they come after you."

"They don't?"

"Uh-uh. Sometimes they make what's called a bluff charge. They'll come roaring at you, but when they get almost up to you, they stop. They'll sniff to find out who you are, then they turn around and go away."

"Gosh!" Angela breathed.

"Yeah! The only problem is, when they're coming at you full speed and woofing their heads off, you can't tell whether they're bluffing or if they're dead serious."

Ant Hil stopped shaking out a pillow to complain, "You make the bears sound like monsters."

"They're not monsters. They're just natural creatures trying to survive in the wild," Becky said, "but the wild keeps shrinking for them. We're on the bears' side! It's for their sake we try to give people the facts."

Ant Hil said, "Your facts are exaggerated."

Becky's face got stiff. She slid off the tailgate and said, "Good-night, folks. Enjoy your evening."

"We need to pay our camp fee," Ant Hil reminded her.

"Oh. Right. My partner Phil said you needed change." She held it out to Ant Hil.

"Do you have to go?" Angela asked.

"Yeah. Phil's going to wonder what happened to me. He'll think I got eaten by a bear." She winked at Angela, then turned to walk down the hill.

The lowering sun stretched the shadows of the lodgepole pines longer and longer as the air grew cool. Ant Hil sniffed deeply. "Doesn't it smell wonderful here?" she asked. "Let's take the sleeping bags out into the trees and lie down. We'll watch the first stars come out."

"I don't think that's a good idea," Angela said. "The ranger said people aren't even allowed to sleep in tents, let alone lie out on the ground."

"I don't mean sleep out there all night," Ant Hil said. "Just experience nature for the rest of the evening. When it gets dark all the way, we'll come back to the truck."

"Okay," Angela said, still dubious. "But we shouldn't go too far."

"You're such a timid old woman sometimes,

Angel." Ant Hil picked up her sleeping bag, which was really Sara's. Even though she had to be quite tired out from the long day's drive, she wouldn't admit it. She would have carried Angela's sleeping bag too if Angela hadn't grabbed it from her.

From outside the woods, the lodgepoles looked as though they grew close together, but inside, there was enough space between trees for the sleeping bags. As the sun set, shining through branches and pine needles, its rays became fragmented like images in a kaleidoscope.

Settled beneath a tree, Ant Hil said, "Lie down and look up, Angel. It's a different perspective. See, the treetops seem to come together like football players in a huddle."

"Uh-huh." Angela didn't look up; she looked around. The woods were empty and still.

"If only we had enough time!" Ant Hil exclaimed. "I'd love to show you all of Yellowstone. The waterfalls, the boiling mud pots . . . "

"You *promised* we'd go home first thing tomorrow morning."

"Yes, I know." She was quiet for a while, then she said, "Angel, just imagine what the ancient Indians must have thought when they saw this place for the first time. How would they have explained to each other the geysers and the boiling pools that stayed hot all winter?"

"I don't know." Angela lay flat on the sleeping

bag, her arms pressed against her sides. Dusk was gathering quickly, dimming the forest.

"From where we are right now, it's as if civilization doesn't exist," Ant Hil went on. "No television or computer games or trucks out here. Let's be totally quiet for a while, Angel, and let ourselves sink into nature."

She tried to do what Ant Hil wanted. At first, everything did seem silent, but then Angela began to notice sounds. Bird calls, the rustle of branches in the wind, and a whistling that repeated again and again. "What's that?" she asked.

"Just little animals. I think they're called whistle gophers. Shhhhhh. Listen."

It got darker. She heard more noises that sounded like creatures moving through the trees. Rolling onto her side, she said, "Ant Hil, I want to go back to the truck. There might be bears out there. The ranger told us—"

Ant Hil's sigh was deep and impatient. "They only try to scare people so that if there should be some minor accident, the visitors can't sue the Park Service. It's all exaggerated. Didn't you see the wink that ranger gave you after she filled your head with those frightening stories?"

So Ant Hil had seen it too. She didn't miss much. "That wasn't what the wink meant," Angela said.

"What did it mean, then?"

How could she tell her that Becky had winked because Ant Hil was a stubborn, maddening, unreasonable old woman? And that after the wink, Angela had given Becky a small nod of agreement. How could she say such a thing to Ant Hil? Even the thought was disloyal. "I don't know for sure," she said.

She lay back and waited. It was really dark now, but not dark enough for the stars to come out. The sounds in the forest grew louder. A branch cracked, and Angela thought she heard a low snuffle, something like a woof coming from far down in a throat. A *big* throat. "I think there's a dangerous animal out there," she said, her voice sliding up in alarm.

"Probably an elk. Elks won't hurt you."

Angela sat up. "Ant Hil, you were wrong about Independence Rock and you were wrong about Old Faithful. You said everything was different now. Maybe you're wrong about the bears, too. Did you ever think of that?" she asked. In another minute she was going to cry. "You *can* be wrong, you know. It's possible."

In the dark, she couldn't see Ant Hil's face, but she heard a short intake of breath. Finally Ant Hil answered, "You're right about everything being different. Especially you. You don't act like my Angel anymore. You're becoming . . . " She paused. It was as if Ant Hil were groping for words in the darkness.

Angela's guilty mind supplied plenty of names

for herself. She was becoming a smart-mouth kid. An ungrateful brat. A rude creep, a no-good monster, a little poop. She didn't know what was happening to herself, either, but she was different, just as Ant Hil said.

With disappointment in her voice, Ant Hil complained, "You're becoming like other children. Pick up your sleeping bag. We'll go back to the truck, if you insist."

15
Night

They were in a car moving away from her, yet she could see their faces. Holding the new baby, they grew smaller and smaller as the car drove off.

"Mommy! Daddy! Come back!" Angela cried in the voice that had belonged to her when she was six years old. "Don't leave me! Please come back!"

But the car kept going. They smiled and waved good-bye, even lifting the tiny hand of the new baby in a farewell wave. She screamed for them to return and take her with them, but they were gone, lost in the distance.

"Angel! Wake up!" She felt someone shake her shoulders. In the blackness she saw no one—only the dream image of her parents and the new baby abandoning her, smiling as they went.

"Dear child! You're having a nightmare. I just knew that ranger was upsetting you with all that talk about bears!"

A nightmare? Then why did it hurt so much? "It wasn't about bears," she cried, not fully awake. "They left me! What did I do wrong?"

"Who left you?"

"My mommy and daddy." She became aware of her own voice channeling into her ears. Her eyes opened onto blackness. Reaching out, she touched Ant Hil, so she knew it was no longer a dream, but the pain still filled her, rolling under her skin. "They're buying a whole house for the new baby," she sobbed, "and they're going to stay home with it when it's born. They didn't do that for me! It's not fair!"

Ant Hil rose to a sitting position and cradled Angela's head in her lap. "Why didn't I see this coming?" she asked. "I couldn't understand what was wrong with you—you've been so moody and strange lately. Now I understand. You're worried about the new baby."

"What if I don't like it?" Angela asked.

"You will."

"How do you know?"

"Because I've been through it. Your grandmother was my baby sister, and I loved her very much."

"That was a long time ago. Everything's different now. You said it yourself."

"Some things don't change." She stroked Angela's hair, which was damp at the temples from tears, and passed gentle fingertips back and forth across her forehead. "Feeling better now?"

"Nooooo!" Angela wailed. "Why did they leave me? Was I bad? Did I cry too much and make fusses?"

Ant Hil hugged her and at the same time gave her a little shake. "Angel, you're talking nonsense. Of course you weren't bad." Fumbling in her purse for a tissue, she said, "Here, dry your eyes. Listen, your parents invested in some oil wells they found out about from people they worked with. When the oil bust came, the investments failed, and they were deeply in debt. You're old enough to know these things now."

Angela sat up so that she and Ant Hil faced each other in the dark, although neither could see much of the other.

"They had to take any jobs they could find to pay off their debts, and it wasn't easy. Finding jobs, I mean. It broke their hearts to leave you."

Angela had stopped crying except for a few delayed sobs that broke out unexpectedly from her chest. "The oil business has been f-f-fine for a long time now," she sniffled. "Why didn't they quit wild-catting sooner so they could come and get me?"

Ant Hil answered slowly, as though she had to choose her words with extra care. "I suppose," she said, "when people have been badly off financially for a while, and then they start making really good money again, they can't bring themselves to stop." She groped in the dark for Angela's hand. "I can't judge your parents, and you shouldn't either. They're trying to make up for it now. If you're smart, you'll let them."

"They didn't buy a house for *me*," Angela accused. "I don't *like* the new baby."

"You'll love it very much, and the baby will love you. Think of all the things you can do together."

"Like what?"

Ant Hil released Angela's hand, then settled once again into her sleeping bag. "Well, for one, you can teach the baby to blow bubbles. You can roll a ball back and forth. Or build a tower of blocks. That's fun."

Oh sure, Angela thought.

Ant Hil's soothing voice went on, "You can blow the fluff off dandelions. My baby sister Margaret used to love doing that. She would laugh so sweetly—I can still hear it. You can count stars together, which you and I never got to do tonight."

"Uh-huh." Angela, too, lay back down in her sleeping bag and slipped her hand under her head.

Drowsily, Ant Hil went on, "Sleep in the back of a pickup truck, like we're doing right now. Read stories. I mean, you'll read to the baby, and teach it the letters of the alphabet. . . . " Her voice faded. Ant Hil had soothed herself back to sleep.

Usually she relied on surprises to distract Angela from pain. Out there in the campground in the middle of the night, Ant Hil couldn't buy a surprise, so she painted rosy pictures with words, thinking that would bluff Angela out of her hurt.

It didn't work. She still felt miserable. The dream picture of her mother and her father and the unborn baby hung in her mind, taunting her. Ant Hil thought she'd figured out what was bothering Angela. The baby. That was part of it—she would have to share her parents when she'd never even had enough of them for herself. But there was a lot more.

There was leaving her friends and moving to a strange city; that was hard. Even worse would be leaving Ant Hil, who shouldn't be left alone, because there was no telling what she might do.

The Alzheimer's seemed to have gone away for a while, at least. Her last craziness had been on Sunday afternoon, and it was now Tuesday. Just barely Tuesday, because it couldn't be too much past midnight.

Angela tossed so much the sleeping bag twisted around her hips. After unzipping it, she got out to straighten it, but bumped her head on the low roof of the camper shell. Ant Hil slept on, undisturbed.

16

Encounter

True to her word, Ant Hil was in the truck and ready to leave by seven-thirty the next morning. "You look awful, Angel," she said. "You have dark shadows under your eyes. Didn't you sleep well after the nightmare?"

"No."

"Well, you'll be back in your own bed tonight."

"Good."

The sun rose, making tree shadows as long as the ones from the evening before, but they stretched in the opposite direction. Ant Hil drove the truck out of the end space on Loop C onto the winding road that passed the ranger cabin. They saw Becky and Phil sitting in a Park Service pickup truck with the motor running, listening to a message on the Park radio.

"Stop, Ant Hil," Angela said. She rolled down her window and called, over the noise of both truck motors, "Good-bye, Becky. Good-bye, Phil."

"It's just as well you're leaving," Becky called

back from the driver's seat of the Park truck. "We may have to close this campground. Someone sighted a grizzly about a half mile from here an hour ago. We're on our way to meet other rangers so we can start a search for it."

"What will you do if you find it?" Angela asked.

Phil leaned across Becky and held up an odd-looking gun with a short, thick barrel. "Knock it out with tranquilizer," he answered.

The Ford slid forward a little; Ant Hil was ready to go. "Wait, Ant Hil. One more thing," Angela called out. "How far is it from here to Casper?"

"About three hundred twenty miles," Becky answered.

Angela must have heard wrong. They couldn't be that far away from Casper. "How much did you say?"

"Three hundred—"

Ant Hil gunned the motor and the Ford roared out onto the highway.

"Three hundred twenty miles!" Angela shouted at Ant Hil. "You said Yellowstone wasn't too far from home! Three hundred twenty miles is *far,* and the way you drive, we won't get there till tonight. I'll miss the whole day of school!"

Evasive, Ant Hil answered, "I wasn't exactly sure about the distance. Anyway, what does it matter if you miss a day? Next year you won't even go to school in Wyoming."

"That's the whole point!" Angela yelled shrilly.

"Oh, never mind! You don't understand anything." She buried her head against her knees. This time she didn't cry. She was too angry for tears.

Almost immediately she felt the truck make a sharp turn, and shortly afterward it pulled to a stop. She uncovered her eyes to look through the windshield. "Why are you stopping? This is a parking lot."

"Well, now, Angel, let's be sensible for a minute. As long as you're going to miss a day of school anyway, why not take an hour or two to see some of the world's most spectacular sights? Right here at Norris Geyser Basin—"

"I don't believe this. I don't believe *you!*" Angela whirled to face Ant Hil. "You're not trying to show me Wyoming. You're just trying to keep me with you as long as you can."

Ant Hil turned away as if she were interested in what she saw through the window. Because of the early hour, only two other vehicles sat in the lot, both of them Park Service trucks. When she turned back she said in a husky voice, "Don't be angry with me. I admit it—I'm selfish where you're concerned. Do you blame me?"

"Yes!" she screamed, and shook the old woman's hand from her arm.

Ant Hil groped around on the seat. "Where's my purse? I need my nasal spray. This pollen . . . "

"There's no pollen! Why do you have to pretend about everything? Just admit it—you're crying!"

"No, I'm not." She sniffed the nasal spray and said, in a quavering, choked voice, "I just can't stand weepy old women!" She kept rummaging in her purse, then opened the door on the driver's side and slid out.

"Where are you going?" Angela demanded.

"To the restroom to take one of my nerve pills. I got a little out of control just now and I apologize. I don't want anything to spoil this happy occasion," she said as she closed the door gently.

Angela scrambled across the seat and rolled down the window as fast as she could. "*What* happy occasion!" she yelled out at Ant Hil's retreating figure. "I'm being held prisoner in a white Ford truck!"

Ant Hil winced, but kept walking toward the restroom. Angela sank back against the seat and pounded the dashboard with her fists.

She hated Ant Hil. No, she didn't, she loved Ant Hil. And Ant Hil loved Angela—too much. That's why she was holding her prisoner. Prisoner of love. That was a song her mother had sung once, when she and Angela's father were joking around in a grimy hotel room somewhere in Louisiana, and Angela had sat cross-legged on a creaky chair laughing at their clowning. But it wasn't funny to be a real prisoner of love. She gnawed her knuckles and tried to figure out if there was any possibility of escape. Before she could think of one, Ant Hil was back.

Standing outside with her arms folded on the

ledge of the open window, she smiled as if nothing had happened. "How's this for a plan?" she asked. "Look down there, Angel." She pointed past the edge of the parking lot to a hilly area thinly covered with lodgepole pines. "Instead of us taking the regular walking tour of Norris Geyser Basin, we'll cut down this slope. From there we might be able to see at least a few geyser pools."

Angela threw up her hands and said, "You just never give up, do you?"

Ignoring her, Ant Hil went on, "As I remember it, one of the thermal fields is right at the bottom. We can get a quick look at it—it shouldn't take more than half an hour. Then we'll get in the truck and drive home." She raised her right hand. "I solemnly promise you I won't make another stop after that, except to buy gas. We won't even stop to eat—we'll just pick up snacks at the gas stations."

Her expression grim, Angela said, "All right. A half hour. That's it! If you break this promise, I'll . . . " She would what? Sulk? Pout? Big wimpy threat!

"I never break promises," Ant Hil said, and seemed to believe she was telling the truth.

There was no real trail to follow, just an open area going into the trees. Thin patches of fresh spring grass grew in the bare spaces between trees. Lodgepole skeletons lay on the ground while other dead trunks tilted crazily, held up by their neighbors.

As she climbed over the fallen limbs on the ground, Ant Hil panted a little. She clutched Angela for balance, but Angela stiffened her arm.

"Look, down there," Ant Hil said. "See the thermal pools?"

From where they stood, the ground beyond the trees appeared barren, swollen with mounds of pale dried mud. Wisps of steam rose from irregularly shaped ponds. "It's lovely in a strange way," Ant Hil said. "Let's go closer so you can get a really good view."

Angela said nothing in reply. She would go along to see the hot pools, but she didn't have to talk. She might never talk to Ant Hil again. A few steps later, though, she was forced to break her silence. "Wait, Ant Hil. I've got a stone in my shoe."

"While you get it out, I'll keep going down the hill because I'm slower than you are. That'll give me a chance to get ahead, so I won't hold you back so much. I don't want to waste time. Half an hour! I promised."

With her shoe in her hand, Angela sat watching Ant Hil labor down the slope. It was steeper than it had looked from the parking lot. Brush and fallen branches made the ground rough. Even from the back, she could tell Ant Hil was breathing heavily. "Slow down!" she called to her.

Angela's jeans and denim jacket were fine for hiking through a forest, but undergrowth kept snagging Ant Hil's sweater and polyester slacks. If going straight down the hill had been a bad idea, Ant Hil would never admit it. She squared her shoulders and marched on. Angela should probably hurry after her to help her, but . . . whose fault was it, anyway, if Ant Hil got herself worn out?

The sight of the thin old woman stumbling through the brush made Angela feel guilty, so she turned to look at the snow-covered mountain peaks in the distance. Something else caught her eye, in the corner of her field of vision. Rising halfway to get a better look through the trees, she gasped. Shock made her drop back down.

Straight across on the slope, fifty feet from her, a grizzly bear stood watching her. He was big— huge!—with a heavy brown coat and a blond streak across his shoulder hump. His massive head swayed from side to side, as if he were trying to get a better look at her, but otherwise he stood still, on all fours.

Angela's heart pounded so wildly she couldn't breathe. She groped for the tree trunk next to her and slowly pulled herself up, never taking her eyes from the bear's. Suddenly he began to come toward her.

Everything Becky had told her flew out of her head like a flock of startled birds. She started to run, but she was wearing only one shoe and she fell.

Sprawled on the ground, she scrambled to her knees and raised her arms over her head. "No!" She could only whisper it, because her voice wouldn't work. Neither Angela nor the bear made a sound.

He couldn't run fast because there was little open space; the trees slowed him into a motion more like a lope. It was a bluff charge. The grizzly only wanted to find out what the creature was. Fifteen feet from her, he stopped and reared up on his hind legs to sniff and get her scent.

Seven feet tall, four hundred fifty pounds, with three-inch claws on front paws held up like a prize-fighter's fists, he looked so enormous and deadly that a scream tore out of Angela's mouth and she kept on screaming. The bear was big enough that if he'd opened his jaws wide, he could easily have crushed her skull. Still, he made no threat, remaining upright on his hind legs. Angela didn't know that bears rarely attack from a standing position. Her screams increased with her terror.

Lower on the slope, Ant Hil whirled around. The instant she saw the grizzly looming over Angela, she remembered exactly what Becky had said: "You absolutely don't run. If you do, a bear will chase you for sure."

"Come after *me!*" Ant Hil shrieked. She jumped up and down and waved her arms, then turned and ran down the hill toward the thermal fields.

Any animal that fled from him showed that it was weaker and would be an easy catch, an easy prey. Responding instinctively, the grizzly chased the old woman. The closer they got to the thermal area, the thinner the trees became, so he could run faster, huffing as he ran. Still more curious than aggressive, he didn't roar, and his ears were only partly laid back.

"Ant Hill!" Angela screamed, trying to run after her but falling again, scraping her hands. It was a much worse nightmare than the night before because she couldn't move fast enough, and she knew she wasn't going to wake up. "Ant Hill!" she shrieked, and tripped and scrambled up again as the bear shortened the distance. Her screams kept her from hearing, at first, the voices behind her.

"There he is! Good lord, he's chasing the old lady! You'll have to free-dart him, Becky. Can you get a clear shot?"

Three rangers ran past Angela, not even slowing to look at her. She recognized Becky and Phil. He shouted, "The old woman's heading out onto the thermal fields! She'll break through the crust!"

The fear in his voice made Angela scramble to her feet and stretch to see. Ant Hil was still running, but staggering now as she reached the bumpy, burned-looking geyser area.

"Hold it, Becky," the other ranger yelled. "Wait a second and you'll have a better chance to hit him. He's not going to go out there. He's too heavy."

At the edge of the thermal field, the grizzly stopped. Again he reared up, watching his prey run to where he wouldn't follow. If he did, the thin crust of earth would break beneath his great weight, letting him sink down into boiling mud and steam, where the heat would quickly kill him. When he heard loud voices behind him he turned, but swiveled his big head once more for a last look at his prey.

"There's a good shot—get him, Becky!"

She fired the dart pistol. The dart, filled with tranquilizer, flew too fast for anyone to see, but the grizzly reared around and tried to bite whatever it was that had stung him on the shoulder. Tense, Becky filled another dart, just in case, although a second dose would kill him.

The grizzly bellowed, and twisted, and waved his front legs so that his claws stood out in sharp outline against the morning sky. Soon he stumbled and fell.

"He's down! Let's go!" the rangers cried.

Angela hadn't waited. Ahead of them, she ran to the rim of the thermal field shouting, "Ant Hil! I'm coming!"

"Grab that kid!" the rangers yelled, and Phil's strong arms caught Angela and pulled her back against his chest. "You can't go out there!" he cried into her ear. "That's dangerous ground. The crust is so thin you could crash right through into boiling mud."

"That's my Ant Hil," she screamed, struggling to get loose. "I have to get her."

"You're not going anywhere. It's not safe out there!"

From the top of the hill, sirens wailed and car doors slammed as additional rangers arrived in response to a radio call. "The bear's out like a light," Becky shouted at them while they raced down the slope. "He'll keep for a while. We've got to get the old lady out of the thermal field."

"I don't know how she even got that far without crashing through the crust," Phil said, holding tightly to Angela, who thrashed in his arms.

"Will it support her?" one of the rangers asked. "If she walked in, maybe she can just walk out."

"Who knows? She could break through the crust any minute and get boiled."

Ant Hil had stopped moving. Steam curled up on all sides of her. Her western hat had fallen when she ran away from the bear; Becky picked it up and stood looking at her helplessly from the edge of the safe ground. "Wouldn't you know," Becky said, "he'd go after the one person in the whole park who wasn't afraid of bears."

Hanging onto Angela but paying no attention to her, Phil said, "Her name's Hilda—we checked her into the campground last night. Call her and see if she'll come out on her own."

"Hilda!" they all began to call, and Angela called, "Ant Hil! Ant Hil!"

"Can you come to us?" the rangers asked. "Come on, Hilda! Just follow the footprints you left in the mud."

As they watched from the edge of the thermal field, Ant Hil slowly stiffened. Her head sank forward. Arms straight at her sides, she became rigid.

"What's the matter with her?" Phil asked.

"Looks like she's in shock or something," Becky said.

"She gets . . . spells," Angela said, her voice breaking, but no one listened to her.

"She isn't responding," the rangers said. "One of us will have to go out there and get her, but . . . " No one knew exactly where the ground surface lay thinnest, covering mud or water heated even beyond the boiling point because of underground pressure.

"I'll go!" Angela yelled, but Phil just tightened his hold on her.

"I weigh less than the rest of you," Becky said quietly. "I volunteer."

"Let me go!" Angela screamed. "I'm not as heavy as Ant Hil! If the ground held her, it'll hold me."

"No way," Becky told her. "You're a child."

"*Let—me—go!*" Angela screamed, kicking Phil's shins with her heels.

"Stop that!" he said. His powerful shoulders and long muscular arms overpowered her. As always. People bigger and stronger and older than she was always controlled her, refusing to let her do what she needed to do.

She slammed her elbows backward into Phil's

stomach. "Oof!" he gasped. The unexpected jab made him loosen his grip for a fraction of a second and she nearly got away, but he grabbed her again and yanked her back to him, crushing her shoulder blades against his chest. In the scuffle, Phil's police whistle flew across Angela's shoulder to hang against her neck. Since it was the only weapon she could reach, she snatched the whistle with her teeth and began to blow, hoping the shrill blasts right next to Phil's ear would torture him enough that he'd let her go. And then . . .

Then she knew what to do.

Short blasts and long blasts. In Morse code, Angela blew: dot dash; dash dot; long dash; dot dot dot; dot dot: dot dash dot dot—*Ant Hil.*

"What's she doing?" the rangers asked. One of them reached out to pull the whistle away from her.

"Leave her alone!" Becky cried. "It's some kind of code."

Sweat broke out on Angela's forehead and her upper lip. She repeated it, spelling out *Ant Hil* again.

Slowly, Ant Hil looked up. Phil slipped off the whistle strap over his head to make it easier for Angela. So scared she could hardly get enough breath to keep blowing the code, she spelled, *Come.* Dash dot dash dot; dash dash dash; dash dash; dot. *Come to me,* and then, after she caught her breath, *I need you.*

Still dazed, Ant Hil frowned, trying to see Angela.

Phil held her only loosely now. Blasting Morse code on the whistle, Angela told Ant Hil to follow the footprints she'd left in the crust. Ant Hil frowned and leaned forward, trying to see the places she'd stepped on her way into the thermal field. She went so slowly that Angela waited in agony, expecting the ground to cave in at any minute and swallow the old woman into heat and boiling mud.

It was a landscape of death she had to cross. Water lay in ponds with strange, eerie colors—lifeless blue patches alternating with grays, rusts, and sulphurous yellows. Steam rose from the irregular surfaces.

A few trees had once grown along the edge of the thermal field, but they'd burned, leaving blackened, twisted limbs. Rocks on the ground were blackened, too, from burning. Dried mud humped around mouths in the earth that breathed out bursts of white steam. The only sign of life was the water boiling and spouting from a number of small geysers.

Step by step Ant Hil came closer. Angela stopped using the whistle and began to cry out, "Here I am, Ant Hil. It's me—Angel. Don't be afraid. Come to me. I need you. I love you."

When at last the old woman reached the safety of solid ground, she collapsed.

17
Lake

They tried to keep her out of the emergency room at Lake Hospital, but Angela wouldn't leave.

"I have to stay with Ant Hil," she insisted. "She saved my life!"

"I heard it was the other way around," the young doctor said. "That you saved her life. Either way, you have a right to stay."

Taking her pulse, listening to her heart with a stethoscope, the doctor bent over Ant Hil, who lay unconscious on a stretcher. "You say you're her great-niece?" he asked Angela. "Maybe you can give us information about this patient. For starts, how old is she?"

"Seventy-eight."

He looked up and asked, "What's she on?"

"On?" She didn't know what he meant.

"Drugs. Medication," he explained. "What has she been taking?"

Angela rummaged through Ant Hil's purse,

then held up the bottle of nerve pills. "These. She took one of these before we walked down the hill."

He examined the bottle, frowned, and said, "These aren't hers. There's a man's name on the label."

"Our neighbor gave them to her—they belonged to the neighbor's husband."

"Who was probably forty years younger and a hundred pounds heavier. What else?" Not waiting for an answer, the doctor grabbed Ant Hil's purse and dumped its contents onto the table. "Nasal spray. Did she use this?"

"When she got stuffed up from the pollen . . . "

"Antihistamines!" he announced, holding up the box of allergy pills for the nurse to see, as if it were a smoking pistol. "How many and how often?" he asked Angela.

"I don't know!" she cried. "If she started to sneeze, she'd swallow one, but she hasn't since we came to Yellowstone."

"Nasal spray and antihistamines by themselves cause confusion in some people," the doctor said. "Did she ever mix them with those tranquilizers?" He pointed to the bottle of nerve pills.

"Yes! At least I think so, that night in the motel. And this morning . . . You mean the pills were what made her act like this?"

"Tranquilizers, antihistamines . . . she's elderly," the doctor explained. "Drugs stay in old people's systems a lot longer. And she's small—what does she weigh, about ninety pounds? Even for great big grizzly bears like the one that chased you, dosages have to be measured out exactly, according to weight. This woman—what's her name? Hilda? She's been taking tranquilizers that are much too strong for her. And then mixing them with nasal spray and antihistamines . . . she could have gotten into serious trouble."

"She did!" Angela cried. "I thought it was Alzheimer's, like Sara's grandmother."

"Start her on an IV," the doctor instructed the nurse. "She may have become dehydrated from the heat on the thermal field. Then . . . " He crossed his arms and for the first time, smiled at Angela. "We'll just have to wait till she sleeps it off. I think she'll be just fine."

Angela burst into tears and buried her head against Ant Hil's neck.

"Here, don't do that!" The nurse pulled her by the shoulders, but Angela clung to Ant Hil. "You'll have to move out of our way so we can begin the IV. Come on, Angela. Why are you crying?"

"Because I'm so h-h—" She took a deep breath. "Happy! That it isn't Alzheimer's."

"This little girl is overwrought," the doctor said. "Let's make her take—"

"No!" Angela whirled on them. Backed against the stretcher like a cornered animal, she shouted, "You can't make me take anything! I won't let you!"

Mildly, the doctor asked, "Not even a nap?

That's all I was going to suggest—that you take a nap. You look like you need one."

"Oh." She nodded, feeling kind of embarrassed about her outburst. "I thought you wanted me to take a drug or something."

He told her, "You can lie down in the same room with your great-aunt while she's sleeping off her overmedication."

She didn't know how long she'd slept or how late it was. Bars of sunlight edged the closed drapes when she woke up, so it couldn't be night. In the dimness of the hospital room she heard voices. Not moving, barely opening her eyes, Angela saw through her lashes that the doctor was sitting on a chair next to Ant Hil's bed.

"What made you think you needed nerve pills?" he asked her. "You don't look nervous to me."

Ant Hil answered very quietly. "It's just . . . I've been depressed." She said it as if it were a crime she wanted to conceal. Angela lay quietly on the bed, breathing softly, not letting on that she was awake, listening to Ant Hil explain, "It's because my grand-niece is moving away from me. I'll hardly ever see her from now on."

"That sounds like a legitimate reason to feel bad," the doctor told her. "I'm still not sure why you thought you needed those pills."

"Knowing I'll be losing her has devastated me. It's torn me apart. I couldn't let the child see that."

"Why not?"

Ant Hil raised herself on one elbow to declare softly, "Childhood is a time of happiness. A child can't understand grief."

"Oh, come on, Hilda," he said. "You know better than that. You're not too old to remember."

It seemed strange to hear the doctor call her "Hilda." He was less than half her age. His hair was thick and reddish, he wore round glasses, and his cheeks were so smooth he looked as if he didn't need to shave every day. Yet he talked to her as if she were a child. And Ant Hil didn't object, didn't correct him, even though she made everyone else call her "Miss Hilda" or "Aunt Hilda" or "Miss McMullen."

"It's okay to feel sad, Hilda," he went on, patting her hand. "You don't have to suppress real feelings with pills."

"I suppose not," she answered, "but I've never worn my emotions out where everyone can see them. From now on, though, I'll keep them under control without pills."

"Control," the doctor said, "is great to have in sports like baseball and bowling."

"And computer games," Ant Hil added.

"In real life," the doctor continued, "too much control, whether it comes from inside you or outside, can be harmful. It causes headaches and bad dreams and other stress-related problems, like chewed knuckles. I noticed Angela's hands."

Angela started to cover her knuckles, but remembered just in time that she was supposed to be sleeping.

"It's just a little habit she has," Ant Hil said.

"She'd be better off if she talked out what's bothering her. So would you. Keeping feelings under too tight a lid can be dangerous."

"Well, thank you for your concern. I'll think about what you've said." Springs squeaked; through fluttering eyelids, Angela watched Ant Hil sit up on the side of the bed. "Now I have to wake up Angel so we can leave. I promised I'd get her back to Casper tonight."

"Do you really think that I would let you leave this hospital and drive all the way to Casper?" the doctor asked her.

"I feel fine now," she insisted. "And I promised Angel."

"I have to admit you look pretty good," he told her, "but that doesn't mean you're in any condition to drive a three-quarter ton truck several hundred miles."

The nurse opened the door then and came into the room. "One of the park rangers is outside. He wants to see Hilda," she announced brightly, not bothering to hush her voice.

That gave Angela the excuse to stretch and yawn

and pretend she'd just awakened. "Hi," she said. "How are you feeling, Ant Hil?"

"Excuse me . . . " Phil poked his head around the door. "Hello," he said. "You're looking better, Miss Hilda. I brought your hat back."

Ant Hil stood up and moved forward, a little shakily, to take the cowboy hat from Phil. "I'm fine," she said. "Just fine. All ready to leave."

"That's what I came about," Phil told her. "Four of us rangers have to be in Denver tomorrow for a conference on grizzly bear management. If the doctor says you can go home, I can drive you and Angela back to Casper in your truck. Tonight. The other rangers will pick me up on their way to Denver."

Angela clutched the edge of the bed. She looked from Phil to Ant Hil to the doctor.

"I haven't released you yet, Hilda," the doctor said.

"I feel wonderful! Being chased by that bear made me realize how much I value my life."

"Then you'd better pay attention to the lecture I'm about to give you," he told her. "Sit down and listen good, okay?"

Obediently, Ant Hil sat on a chair next to the door, where Phil waited.

Clearing his throat, the doctor spoke sternly. "Hilda, has anyone ever told you how dangerous it is to take other people's medications? Not only was

139

the dosage of those nerve pills much too strong for you, but you were mixing them with things they shouldn't have been mixed with."

She answered, "I got the allergy pills and nasal spray at the drugstore. They were just to stop my sneezing."

"If you'd gone to your doctor," he told her, "he'd have given you safer medicines that wouldn't have reacted against each other."

"She," Ant Hil said.

"What?"

"She. My doctor's a woman." She smiled as if she'd caught him in a slipup.

He reddened a little. "Are you taking this seriously?" he asked, peering at her through his round glasses. "I feel like I'm not getting through to you, Hilda. What I'm trying to tell you is extremely serious," he said. "Deadly serious."

Deadly is right. She nearly killed us both, Angela thought. The image of that tractor trailer coming closer and closer would stay in Angela's mind always. She stood up and said in a no-nonsense voice, "Ant Hil, I want you to pay attention to what he's saying. Okay?"

"Thanks, Angela," the doctor said. "Hilda, if I agree to let you leave the hospital, you have to promise me you'll see *her,* your own doctor, in Casper tomorrow. In fact, I'm going to phone her so she'll expect you."

"I promise," Ant Hil said, looking first at the doctor, then at Angela. The smile had disappeared.

"Don't worry, I'll make sure she goes," Angela told him.

"Good. Excellent. And Hilda, promise me also that you'll never again take a prescription that belongs to someone else. I'm going to keep your medicines here," he told her. "I don't even want you to have them with you."

"What if I sneeze on the way to Casper?"

"Use a handkerchief." He got up and went to the door. "Good-bye, Hilda. I'll sign the papers so you can leave."

Ant Hil stared soberly at the door swinging closed behind the doctor. Then, turning to Phil, she said, "Bless you for offering to drive us home. I don't think I could have managed it."

Ant Hil admitting she couldn't do something? Angela was amazed.

Phil answered, "I'll drive you home only on one condition. Angela has to promise not to kick me again." He grinned at Angela.

Startled, Ant Hil asked, "She kicked you? My Angel?"

"For sure. When she was trying to run out and rescue you, your angel acted more like a wildcat. I've got bruises on my shins to prove it."

"Sorry," Angela said, but she couldn't keep the happiness from spreading over her face. They were going home tonight! She could go to school tomorrow.

"I just want to make one stop on the way," Phil said.

"Oh, no!" Angela groaned. Not again!

Phil said, "I hope it's not a problem. It's just that. . . Becky wants to say good-bye."

They found her sitting on a railing beside a bear trap. Made of culvert pipe, the trap rested on wheels and had a trailer hitch at one end.

"Want to see him?" she asked. "The bear that chased you? We gave him an extra sedative so he wouldn't go crazy and try to tear up the trap. He's pretty quiet right now."

"Yes! I want to see him."

Angela got out of the truck, but Ant Hil said, "I think I'll just stay in here. I'm still a little tired."

The front end of the trap was secured by a heavy steel gate. Angela went right up to it and looked in. Only inches from her she saw a massive brown head. The eyes, level with hers, looked straight at her. She thought she'd be afraid, but she wasn't, even though she stood so close that her breath made small ripples in the fur on his face.

"He's a magnificent animal," Becky said.

"What's going to happen to him?" Angela asked.

Phil told her, "He'll get a nice ride into the back

country, dangling from a cable underneath a helicopter, but he'll never know it because he'll be asleep through the whole thing. Before we let him go, we'll put a radio collar on him. That way we can track him and make sure he doesn't try to come back to the people areas of the park."

"What if he does?"

Above Angela's head, Becky and Phil exchanged glances.

"Sometimes bears get too fond of people food," Becky answered slowly. "They have fantastic memories, so it's hard to change their habits. If this griz turns out to be like that, one that won't give up his taste for picnic lunches . . . "

In the cage, the grizzly had lifted one front foot so the long claws came through the bars. Halfheartedly, he scratched the bars as if he knew it would do no good.

"I mean, I sure hope it doesn't happen that way," Becky continued, "but if he comes back into the visitor areas one or two more times, he'll have to be removed from the population."

"What does that mean?" Angela asked.

Phil busied himself picking a spot of mud off his uniform. He muttered, "Bear heaven."

"You mean, kill him?"

Becky said, "It's not something we want to do, believe me. But we can't have grizzlies invading people territory."

Indignant, Angela cried, "That's not fair! It seems to me it's the people who are invading grizzly territory! The bears were here first, weren't they?"

"You sure are a smart girl, Angela," Becky said. "When you get older, think about joining the Park Service."

"Maybe I will," Angela answered.

"You get great benefits, like these fabulous designer uniforms . . . . " Becky laughed when she said that. "Nice low pay . . . " Then she became serious. "And a chance to help endangered animals survive."

"Yeah," Phil agreed, "that's the best part of it. So keep in touch with us while you're growing up. For now, though, we better get back into the truck. It's a long drive to Casper."

Angela held out her hand to Becky, who squeezed it in farewell. "Becky," she asked, "did you make that strap Phil's whistle is on?"

"Yes, I did. It's called a lanyard. Do you like it? Do you want it? I can make him another one."

"Here," Phil said, lifting it from around his neck and slipping it over Angela's head. "Might as well take the whistle, too. Keep it as a souvenir."

Angela lingered for one last, long look into the cage.

"Please," she begged the grizzly, "stay away from people. I want you to live."

18

Choices

The last day. When the final bell rang, the kids cheered. Like beads pouring through a funnel, they bunched around the school doors and burst forth into the freedom of summer.

Angela expected her friends to linger in the schoolyard with her to bid their last farewells, but no one did. Not even Sara. Everyone must have been in too big a hurry to get home, kick off shoes and school clothes, and pull out shorts, soccer balls, skateboards, and scooters.

Clutching her disappointment against her chest behind her notebook, she had the feeling that she'd already become history in Casper. It hurt. Then she saw Ant Hil waiting for her on the sidewalk.

"What are you doing here?" Angela asked. "Today isn't Wednesday."

"I just saw my allergy doctor, and I'm on my way to pick up some prescriptions. I thought maybe you'd walk to the drugstore with me."

"Okay." Might as well, since there was no one to hang out with.

Ant Hil handed Angela a letter and said, "This came in today's mail for you."

She expected it to be from her parents, but the handwriting looked too bold and square. The return address was Spotted Horse, Wyoming. Larry! She'd given him her address, but she hadn't expected him to write so soon, if at all! She flushed with pleasure.

"Aren't you going to open it?" Ant Hil asked.

"Later." She would when she was alone. She tucked the letter into her notebook, and matched her steps to the clicking heels of Ant Hil's sensible brown shoes.

Inside the drugstore, the pharmacist said, "Miss Hilda, you need to take these capsules one hour before meals, on an empty stomach. Now the pink pills have to be taken *with* meals, or they might upset your digestion. And if your vision should become blurry, discontinue this prescription immediately."

"The pink ones?"

"No, Miss Hilda, the capsules. Can you keep that straight?"

Ant Hil drew herself up and smiled confidently. "Of course I can. Pink pills an hour before meals . . ."

"No, Miss Hilda. The other way around."

They left the drugstore and had walked partway home when Ant Hil looked at her watch and said, "Let's sit on this bus-stop bench for a few minutes."

"Why? Is something wrong?"

"Angel, for heaven sakes, you're such a worry-wart. I just want to sit down. Do you have to make a big fuss over every little thing I do or say? I'm perfectly fine now, I promise you."

Angela paced in front of the bench and said, "How can you expect me not to worry about you? Tomorrow my mother and dad are coming. Two days after that we're leaving for Texas."

"Right. And it's going to be just wonderful for you to live with your parents and the baby in El Paso."

She stopped pacing to stand in front of Ant Hil. "Texas can't be wonderful for me if you're still in Wyoming. You'll be all alone. What if you take the wrong pills? Or you could fall, or something."

Ant Hil said, "My dear child, I've been perfectly safe in Wyoming for seventy-eight years."

"Safe!" Angela almost yelped with frustration. "It was Wyoming where you nearly wrecked the truck! And got chased by a bear!"

"You won't need to worry about my safety if I stay in my own house, will you?" Ant Hil asked. "I'll be fine! Really!"

Angela sat on the curb and looked up at her. With the sun behind her, her gray hair shone silver, like a halo. "You know, Ant Hil," she said, "you've got to be the stubbornest person in Casper. Maybe in Wyoming. Probably in the whole United States."

"Now that *is* an exaggeration." She smiled.

"When I was little," Angela went on, "I used to pretend the tablecloth was a magic web that would protect me from bad things. But it couldn't. Your house can't protect you either."

"But it can." Gently, Ant Hil nodded, as if she had a whole lifetime of wisdom and experience inside her that Angela couldn't be expected to understand.

"There's something I wasn't going to tell you," Angela said with a sigh. "I thought I'd keep it a secret, but now I've changed my mind." She took Ant Hil's hand and stared straight into her eyes. Then she told her about the four burners blazing in the kitchen on the evening of their Thanksgiving celebration, how possible it was that a fire could have started to destroy the house and maybe the three people inside.

"Oh, no! Did I really do that?" Ant Hil buried her face in her hands.

"Yes. And all the other scary things I've already told you about. You did them." She pulled Ant Hil's fingers away from her eyes. "It isn't where you are that keeps you safe. It's who you're with. I want you with me in El Paso. I need you as much as you need me."

For the first time, Ant Hil seemed to waver. "If I went, who would take care of my house?"

"Neighbors. We'd make arrangements. And every year you and I could come back here to spend the whole summer in your house."

"You'd have to ask your parents. They might not let you."

"I'll ask," Angela said, "but I know they'll say yes. Anyway, I'm nearly twelve. I'm old enough to make some choices of my own."

Ant Hil looked at her watch. "My gracious, it's getting late. We have to go home."

Angela stood unmoving, blocking Ant Hil so she couldn't get up from the bench. "You're stuck there till you give me your answer," she said.

"What answer?"

"Yes. That's the only answer I'll take. Yes, you'll come and live with us in El Paso."

Ant Hil looked up and said, "If it's the only way I can get you to move, I'll say yes."

"*Yes?* Do you mean it?"

"I mean it."

Angela pulled her to her feet. "Really! You'll come to Texas?"

"Really. If you and I can return here every summer."

"Wow! I can't believe it!" Angela yelled and jumped and clapped her hands, then grabbed Ant Hil and whirled her around in a dance right on the sidewalk, not caring that an old man walking past laughed out loud at them. "That's super! It's great! Fantastic! I can't wait to tell Mom and Dad!"

"Let's get home now," Ant Hil said. She started off at such a brisk clip that Angela had to run to catch up. Both of them took little skips along the sidewalk as they went, from pure joy.

"You know," Angela told her, "you were right about one thing, Ant Hil. Wyoming is a beautiful state. I'm sorry I was too grouchy to enjoy it. I wish we could do the trip over again."

"We can!" Ant Hil cried. "Every summer we can travel through Wyoming. There's so much to see . . . there's the big rodeo in Cheyenne . . . you'd love that, Angel!"

"Sounds great! Next summer?"

"Yes! Let's do it. And it won't be many more summers before you're old enough to drive."

They'd reached their house and climbed the steps to the porch. Ant Hil threw open the front door.

"Surprise!" Kids burst from the kitchen and dining room into the living room—Heather and Krystal and Jeffrey and Staci and Terri and dozens of others. In front of them all stood Sara, who threw a handful of confetti into the air. Most of it fell back down on Sara herself, peppering her dark curls with bright tiny dots.

"What took you so long, Miss Hilda?" Sara asked. "Everyone's been here for half an hour."

Frozen with surprise, Angela stood in the doorway until her friends grabbed her arms and pulled her into the dining room. "Look at the cake!" they yelled. "Presents, too."

"I won't tell you what I got you," Sara said.

"Yes, I will! Press-on nails and your own bottle of 'Crimson Claws.' "

Boxes wrapped with bright paper and decorated with enormous bows circled a huge cake shaped like the state of Texas. A message in icing spelled "Goodbye, Angela. We'll miss you." Crepe-paper streamers twisted across the ceiling. The boys batted balloons back and forth; the loud bangs when they burst raised the noise level even higher as everyone crowded around, tugging at Angela and trying to talk to her at the same time. "Did you guess?" "Were you really surprised?" "Did you wonder where we all went after school?"

Angela wanted to cry and laugh at the same time, but mostly she just felt wonderful. As soon as she could free herself from her friends, she threw her arms around Ant Hil, who said, "Well, I guess everyone likes surprises, don't they?"

"The best was the one you gave me back there on the bench!" Angela said. Her friends surrounded her then, to shower her with more balloons, more confetti, and school pictures of each of them so she wouldn't forget Wyoming.

As if she ever could.

GLORIA SKURZYNSKI first went to Yellowstone National Park to see the bears. Later, she returned to interview rangers for her nonfiction book *Safeguarding the Land*. She revisited Yellowstone while researching *Dangerous Ground* so that she could investigate her settings and talk to the rangers about the behavior of the park's bears.

The fires of 1988 broke out as she was completing her manuscript, and she kept in close touch with subsequent events. When the fires ended she revised her manuscript, consulting with rangers so that she could include the most accurate descriptions possible of the changed environment.

While this novel marks her Bradbury Press debut, Ms. Skurzynski has written more than fifteen stories for young people, including the Christopher Award-winning *What Happened in Hamelin*. As a transplanted easterner, she is especially pleased that *Lost in the Devil's Desert* won the Utah Children's Book Award and that *Trapped in the Slickrock Canyon* won the Golden Spur Award, awarded by the Western Writers of America.

With the publication of this new novel, *Dangerous Ground,* Gloria Skurzynski salutes the state of Wyoming on its centennial celebration.

The author lives in Salt Lake City, Utah.